Gisela Bohnstedt-Hannon

If it all changes
an Autobiography

Bibliographic information of the German National Library: The German National Library lists this publication in the German National Bibliography; detailed bibliographic data is available on the Internet at dnb.dnb.de.

Publisher: BoD · Books on Demand GmbH, Überseering 33, 22297 Hamburg, bod@bod.de

Print: Libri Plureos GmbH, Friedensallee 273, 22763 Hamburg

ISBN: 978-3-8192-4734-7
Original German title: *Wenn es anders kommt*
Translated by Peter Hannon with the help of DeepL
Typesetting and Layout: Peter Hannon with VivaDesigner®
Typeset in Palatino Linotype
Cover: Image by 14213153 from Pixabay
Autorenportrait: Arne Houben

Sometimes the path only becomes clear when you start walking it.

Paul Coelho, Brazilian author

Foreword

Life is a story of development and begins with childhood. What shapes us? What are our goals in life? Can we realize them? Do we have the opportunities and the strength to overcome obstacles? Do we learn to distinguish between lies and truth, or do we allow ourselves to be deceived and misled?

Throughout our lives, people and situations make us think and hopefully give us the chance to become the person we always wanted to be.

This autobiographical novel does not claim to be universally valid. It is the life story of a woman and her testimony of 40 years in the GDR.

The personalities and events mentioned are real; the dialog is partly invented.

Chapter I – Childhood

My parents and grandparents

My parents had a very difficult life, which I know from stories and have partly experienced myself. They both came from poor backgrounds.

My grandfather was killed in the First World War and left behind a widow with 6 children. My father was the youngest. My grandmother died during the Second World War when my father was taken prisoner.

I only got to know the grandparents on my mother's side.

This grandfather came back from the First World War with a wooden leg and met my grandmother in the military hospital, where she did simple unskilled labor. My mother was the eldest of 5 siblings. In 1938, at the age of 17, she married my father, who was 5 years older. My brother was born a year before the outbreak of the Second World War. My father had to go to war in 1939 and the young family was separated for the next 7 years. My mother not only had to look after her own child, but also her four siblings, as her mother was ill all her life. My father was seriously wounded in the war on the Eastern Front. Shrapnel had drilled into his body. He was sent to a military hospital in Hamelin and was then sent to the Western Front with a shortened leg. In 1944, my mother received a missing person's report. It turned out that my father had been captured by the Americans in Normandy and was in a prisoner of war camp in Boston. Fortunately, he returned home in August 1946.

That gave me the chance to be born. He was scarred by the war and was in pain for the rest of his life. Many relatives and friends had died in the war or perished in the bombing raids. My parents didn't talk much about it, they didn't want to look back. When I was born, I already had a 9-year-old brother. My mother was 26 and my father 31 years old. They were still young enough to make the best of their lives.

Political situation

After the victory over Hitler's Germany, the country was divided into four occupation zones by the Allies.

I was born in Königsaue, a village in the Soviet-occupied zone. The village no longer exists today. It was bulldozed in the 1960s for brown coal. I was 2 years old when the Western Allies founded the Federal Republic of Germany on May 23, 1949, with the initially provisional seat of government in Bonn and Konrad Adenauer as its first president.

On October 7, 1949, the GDR was founded in the Soviet-occupied zone, which meant the division of Germany. The first and only president of the GDR was Wilhelm Pieck.

As a small child, of course, I knew none of this. I grew up in a part of the country that became increasingly isolated from the world over time.

Early childhood

I only have good memories of my childhood. They take place in a green landscape, with a wide blue sky, fruit trees, spoil heaps and lots of playmates. I was a happy child.

In 1950, when I was three years old, my parents got a small new apartment in a 15-family house built especially for miners at the end of the village. I still remember the move. We drove down the long Aschersleben road in Farmer Wahle's horse-drawn cart and the trailer behind us was loaded with furniture. I sat on the coachman's seat with my father and looked down at the two broad horses' backs. My parents were overjoyed to finally have a heated apartment. I no longer had to sleep in an unheated room with gloves and a hat on. Anyone who worked in the shaft was given a deposit of briquettes and a few liters of shaft schnapps, which they always gave to my grandpa Holzbein[1].

We lived in the large shaft house with the neighbors almost like in a commune. There were three entrances for five families each. You had to follow the house rules and coordinate with the neighbors. The hallway, cellar, attic and yard had to be kept clean. A key was always handed out for this purpose. If you wanted to use the washhouse, you had to sign in on a roster.

Everything was limited to the bare necessities of the time and there was no question of modern living. There was neither a bathroom nor a toilet in the apartment, only a tap in the hallway.

As there was no bathroom in any of the apartments, the washhouse was used on Saturdays for children's bathing. If you were too big for the small zinc bathtub, you could also go to the shaft and use a bathtub in the miners' washhouses for 50 pfennigs. However, you couldn't sit in it for as long as you wanted, as there were usually other villagers waiting who also wanted to treat themselves to the luxury of a bath.

To get to the toilets, the so-called outhouses, you had to cross the courtyard to a smaller building, which also included the wash house, the stables and the hayloft. Every entrance to the house had such a building. Behind it were stables to keep chickens, rabbits and other domestic animals. In the beginning, my parents also had a goat.

When I went to school, my mother started working in the mine shaft and was given one housekeeping day a month, which she needed it in order to do the laundry. She soaked

1 Wooden leg

everything in tubs and containers the evening before. The work clothes were always particularly dirty from the coal dust. Everything was pre-washed first before it was put into the large washing kettle filled with suds, under which there was a coal stove that always had to be refilled. The laundry in the boiler was slowly heated and moved back and forth with a wooden rotating spindle. My mother would then take pieces out of the kettle one by one, place them in a wooden tub and work on them with a brush and washboard. I hated washing clothes. My mother couldn't get me to do the washing of handkerchiefs on the washboard. She never forced me to do anything I didn't like.

Laundry was hung out in the large courtyard between the washhouse and the house in both summer and winter. Wooden laundry supports were placed under the lines so that the laundry could flutter high in the wind and dry faster. In winter, it was sometimes scary when the frozen pants and jackets moved up and down and rattled in the wind. There were clothes drying racks in the yard all year round. When I was learning to ride a bike, I once hit a clothes horse, tipped over and banged my knee. But clothes horses were very good for building stilts and it was great fun to run around the yard with them later on.

Our apartment was about 50 square meters and had two bed-rooms and a kitchen-living room. I initially shared a room with my older brother, but when he went into an apprentice-ship at the age of 15 and only came home at weekends, I had the room to myself.

We didn't have much, a bed for everyone, a shared closet, a table, 4 chairs and a stove with removable iron rings. My brother had once shown me how to make potato peels spin on the stove. He peeled the skin off a potato so that it looked like a spiral, attached it to the upper part of a wooden skewer and stuck the lower part into the potato, which he then placed on the hot oven plate. It looked very pretty as the potato spiral turned around the skewer. However, my father suddenly came into the room and the game was over. He shouted at my brother and slapped him in the face. "Do you have to show her such nonsense!" Later, I secretly showed other playmates the trick. There were often arguments between my brother and my father. It was probably because they had been separated from each other for too long due to the war and my brother saw me as competition.

There were only a few games I played with him. He usually tricked me or made fun of me: "Bet you can't repeat that? Say it really quickly: Hirsch heiß ich[2]." Then he would laugh at me: "You're probably a pig!" When he wanted to eat my pudding, he would distract me: "Look, there's a big bird on the roof." I usually fell for it and lost out. He was going through puberty and only ever wanted to roam around with his friends of the same age. His little sister was a nuisance. I can't remember him looking after me even once.

My parents worked from the moment they got up until they went to bed. After the morning shift in the pit and a simple lunch at home, they usually went to the allotment or to a rented plot of land where they grew fruit and vegetables or potatoes. They looked after the chickens, rabbits and goats. The additional self-sufficiency was necessary because what they got from the ration cards was not enough to live on. You needed barter goods or extra money to buy special things, such as butter or honey. The ration cards were only abolished in the GDR in 1958, when I was 11 years old. In West Ger-

---

2 My name is Hirsch. Spoken quickly it is unpleasant.

many, this had already happened in 1950, as a result of the Marshall Plan. While the Soviet Union insisted on reparations payments as compensation for the war and removed businesses and railroad tracks, the USA supported the western post-war countries with loans and aid deliveries. In the GDR, the aim was to improve living conditions by increasing working performance in line with the Soviet model. To this end, Adolf Hennecke launched a movement that focused primarily on increasing benefits in the mining industry. Naturally, the working population was not enthusiastic about the demand for higher benefits while working and living conditions remained poor. In 1953, there was a popular uprising throughout the country, which was quickly put down by the deployment of Soviet tanks and police units. There were also riots in the Königsauer Schacht. As a child, I didn't notice any of this, only that gradually more and more of my classmates were absent.

In addition to his work in the shaft, my father also wove wicker baskets for the farmers, worked as a handyman for the roofer and went hamster trapping. I often gave the hamster and rabbit skins to Mr. Sonntag in the village and got a few pennies for them, sometimes even a mark, which I handed in at home. My mother also earned extra money by sewing clothes for other people or working as a washerwoman. Despite all the work, my parents were always in a good mood, because for them work also meant balance and relaxation. They were happy when everything thrived in the garden. Mother loved flowers more than anything. That's why asters, dahlias and Bleeding Hearts bloomed in the front garden.

At harvest time, her mother often sat together with other neighbors' wives on the large farm. They chopped home-grown beans or carrots, cut up apples or pitted cherries, depending on what needed to be processed. They told stories and sometimes sang songs: "Am Brunnen vor dem Tore"[3] or "Im schönsten Wiesengrunde"[4]. My mother was a very good housewife, she cooked, baked, pickled cucumbers, made sauerkraut and made balloons for redcurrant wine in the cellar. My parents had a strict daily routine, but it left me a lot of freedom. It was important to my parents that I always studied and did my homework. I was only involved in the housework to a limited extent. I was only allowed to help with the shopping. I was given a shopping list and ration cards. Then my mother sent me out, usually on Saturday, on the bike that my father had put together from old parts.

I knew my way around the village and the villagers knew me too. I loved shopping, got milk from Mrs. Breiche, sausage and meat from Kinne the butcher, muckefuck[5], flour and margarine from Bremer the grocer and bread from one of the bakers, Brachvogel or Rust.

When I remember my childhood, I know what it's like to have a home. Everyone knows you and you know everyone. I still have the village map in my head and know what most people's names were and where they lived. Festivals were organized in the village and people celebrated together. In Königsaue there was the annual miners' festival, with a parade, dancing and children's games such as sack races, egg races and maypole climbing. Once, as a ten-year-old, I even went on stage and sang "Chico Charlie". The villagers applauded and said I would definitely become a pop singer one day. I loved singing and was also in the school choir. My parents bought me a mandolin and I was soon playing in

---

3 At the well outside the gate
4 In the most beautiful meadow
5 Coffee substitute

8

a mandolin group in the village with Mr. Kersten. But I wasn't really interested in becoming a star and I found reading music far too strenuous. The most impressive thing was the 200th anniversary celebrations in 1953. Everyone was proud of our village, which had been founded by the Prussian King Frederick II, known as Old Fritz. The inhabitants made a real spectacle of it, dressing up as cossets and farmers, just as their ancestors had looked back then, driving through the village in Palatinate covered wagons and dancing through the village streets in traditional costumes. The festival lasted for a few days and there was probably no one who didn't take part. Even a storyteller was organized for the children, which I particularly enjoyed.

My parents couldn't afford to go on vacation. At that time, there were only 14 days of vacation a year. I usually spent the summer vacations at children's holiday camps, in the Harz Mountains, in Thuringia, at the Müritz or on the Baltic Sea, sometimes also with my Aunt Ella in Ballenstedt, where there were two younger cousins.

I remember once traveling with my parents on the train to Magdeburg to visit Uncle Ernst and Aunt Anni. They lived at Ostrowskistraße 89 and I must have been about 4 years old. Anni was a cousin of my mother. On the train from Aschersleben we had to open our umbrellas because the roof of the carriage was leaking and it was raining cats and dogs. Aunt Anni had given me a tiny little doll's pram with a doll, which I pulled behind me on a ribbon.

The trolley with the little doll often fell over on the bumpy foot-paths and the adults waited patiently until I had collected everything again. At some point, my father took me in his arms and said: "Look up there!" Magdeburg was one of the cities most destroyed by the war, in comparison even worse than Dresden,

Cologne or Berlin, and it took several years for everything to be rebuilt. That was the first time I saw a ruin from the war, a large bombed-out house. The gable end had been torn open and I could see into a sooty room where there was still a single table. I have kept the image in my memory.

Sometimes my mother would tell me a bedtime story or sing me a song. I loved listening to the song "Schlaf ein, schlaf ein, mein Kindelein"[6]. She sang it very sensitively. It wasn't until much later that I understood why it was so close to me and what this song must have really meant to her.

„ Wenn andere Mädchen zum Balle gehen und springen,
dann muss ich an der Wiege stehen und singen:
Schlaf ein. Schlaf ein, mein Kindelein,
wo mag denn nur dein Vater sein?
Da weinte das Mädel so sehr."[7]

My brother once told me that our mother had often sung this song to him during the war when he was still small.

When I was alone in the apartment during my parents' night shift, I was sometimes frightened. It could happen that the floral pattern on the curtains turned into horrible ghosts and I had to crawl under the quilt. Sometimes the ghosts' heads would flash brightly and then jump all over the four walls. This actually meant that my father was passing by with the electric locomotive. He had explained it to me and said that I didn't need to be scared, but I was anyway.

When I once told my mother about the ghosts in the curtains, she took me to the large country store in Breite Straße, the

---

6 Go to sleep, go to sleep, my little child
7 *When other girls go to the ball and jump,*
then I have to stand at the cradle and sing:
Go to sleep. Go to sleep, my little child,
where might your father be?
The girl cried so much.

building where the Löffler inn used to be. You could buy a lot of things there now, because Königsaue had become a central place.

My modest mother told the sales clerk that she wanted to buy curtains for her bedroom. The saleswoman's reply still rings in my ears today: "The curtains should match the bed frame. What color is your bed frame?" We didn't have a bed surround. Firstly, it was a luxury item by our standards and secondly, the bedroom was so small that not even a bed surround would have fitted in. Even the bedside cabinets had to stand on top of the closet. I felt so sorry for my mother. I don't remember what she said. She then bought a light green fabric and sewed the curtains at home.

Although I grew up as an only child, I never felt alone. I had no problems making friends and my playmates were boys and girls. We played soccer, built potato pits or climbed trees; played with dolls or marbles or played circle games, father-mother-child or hide-and-seek. I was never bored. There was always something interesting to discover. You met children everywhere when you went out into the yard or the street. Shortly before Easter, I collected fuel for the Easter bonfire on the Osterberg with other children. We went through the village with a handcart and rang the farmers' doorbells. We were happy about every old tire we could get hold of. Rubber tires would burn like hell.

In May, we went out with buckets of water and shook cock-chafer beetles off the maple trees in Ascherslebener Straße. We used them to feed the chickens, who greedily pounced on them. Supposedly they laid more eggs as a result. In winter, we usually went sledging or skiing. The Mühlberg was the best place for downhill runs. In the autumn, you could collect chestnuts and make animals out of them.

I didn't go to kindergarten and later I didn't go to after-school care either. Perhaps I was very lucky that not everything was so well organized in those years.

I think the whole village was my home at times. I had lots of school friends who took me home with them after school. My parents actually always wanted me to go home straight after school and do my homework. But that hardly ever happened. My friends usually had a mother or grandmother at home and I was allowed to eat with them after school: Himmel und Erde[8], plum dumplings, black sour or swede soup. While playing afterwards, I regularly forgot the time to get home on time. When my parents came home from their early shift at around 2.30 p.m., they often had no choice but to look for me all over the village. I could be anywhere, at Maria's in the vicarage, at Gudrun's in the Gasthaus zum goldenen Stern, at Helga's in the mayor's house, at Ingrid's, whose father was a teacher and grandfather a painter, or at Erika's on the Neubauern farm. My parents had to scold me a lot, but the drama kept repeating itself. However, I always did my homework and there were never any nasty entries in my diary.

When I played with the neighbor's children, whose parents also worked shifts, it often didn't end well. We were a small, close-knit group of 7 children: Richard, Ute, Eckhard, Rainer, Bernd, Raimund and me. Without supervision, we did a lot of nonsense in our naivety. Once we played hide and seek in the cornfield and trampled all the grain into crop circles. A storm couldn't have done such a bad job. Afterwards, our parents had to pay compensation to the farmer who had suffered the damage.

---

8 Himmel und Erde (Heaven and Earth) is a traditional German dish of mashed potato with stewed apples or pears. In Cologne it is frequently served with sliced blood sausage.

Another time we played Indians and made a small campfire. The wind carried a spark away into the big straw straw. It caught fire and the fire department had to put it out. Our parents had to pay for that too.

We secretly stole our mothers' umbrellas and played parachute jumping on the heels of the coal mine. The wind blew underneath and broke the poles. Our mothers suffered the damage.

Richard was the instigator of all nonsense. He was the eldest, who also taught us how to smoke with a puff. He had bought Muck cigarettes from the kiosk, supposedly for his father. He explained to us how to do it properly: pull hard on the cigarette, as if inhaling, then swallow the smoke and exhale it through your nose. There would then be a lot of smoke curls. It was not intended that this would make us sick.

From then on, our parents forbade us to play with Richard. He was later sent to the youth work camp because he was difficult to bring up, but he had actually always been a good playmate with great ideas. Unfortunately, he lost his father as a child when he fell off a ridge in an excavator. I will never forget those childhood years and I still feel sorry today for what happened to Richard.

But the way life was and the way it developed, it was normal for me. My childhood was an adventurous time, without control and restrictions.

But didn't it later have to become a conflict when I realized the contrast between feeling free and being locked up?

My godmother, Grete

I still remember how I once drove all alone in a doll's pram along a country road to visit Aunt Grete and my great-grand-mother. I was just 3 years old. It was a beautiful day. The sun was shining, but my parents were still fast asleep. First I looked at the picture book I knew by heart, where Katrinchen visits her grandmother: "You can joke over milk and cake" it said. I liked that. I got dressed and set off with the doll's pram. I knew the way to Winningen along the 3 km long country road, because my father had often taken me on his shoulders when we walked there. Aunt Grete had given me the baby doll in the doll's pram. On the way, I picked a bunch of flowers from a cornfield. It had been the same in the picture book. Strangely enough, I didn't meet anyone. It must have been very early in the morning.

I arrived safely at Aunt Grete's and great-grandmother's house, but neither of them were very happy and there was no milk and cake. Aunt Grete was very agitated and borrowed a bicycle basket, put me in it, strapped the doll's pram onto the back seat and immediately drove me back home. My parents were stunned, but overjoyed. They had already missed me and had looked for me everywhere in the village. But no one had seen me, which wasn't really surprising.

The walks to Aunt Grete's soon disappeared forever, because there was no way to get to the West.

In the 1950s, she had gone to the West with her grown-up children Liselotte and Werner.

She was no longer able to accompany me on the rest of my life's journey.

Mr. Goerns

The child's paradise was gradually destroyed. I can still see myself standing in front of the school building with my classmates from Year 1. The Easter vacations were over. We were happy to see our teacher again, whom we loved dearly. Most of the children were brought to school by their mothers, holding hands. The bell had long since rung for lessons. But our teacher didn't show up. I wonder if he was ill. Hopefully nothing had happened to him. He always came from the neighboring village on his bike. He usually took me to school on the back seat because he passed our house anyway and I had the longest way to school from class. My mother had been wondering that morning. She hadn't seen him today. Then she had taken me to school. Now we found out. We cried until our eyes hurt, everyone cried, the children and the mothers. We couldn't believe it. Our beloved Mr. Goerns had left. He would never come back. Why had he done that? Had he not thought of us children at all? How could he leave so easily? We all loved him so much.

One day, the school desk in the row in front of me was also empty. The quiet, clever Martin, my first secret great love, Martin, who had shared his only chewing gum from the West with me and who had not yet known that I wanted to marry him one day, had disappeared one day with his parents to the West. An old school picture shows that he really did exist. He never found out about my childhood dreams. I'm sure he forgot about me at some point. He will never have known that he or his parents hurt me very much.

There were also Volker, Bodo and Bärbel and many others, whose names I have since forgotten, who were suddenly no longer there.

Nevertheless, not everything was just a series of sad experiences

15

for me. Children create their own fantasy world and are known to play and laugh even in times of war or in concentration camps. Many of my former compatriots would now object: You can't compare that and it wasn't that bad in the GDR either. They had many wonderful experiences as pioneers and would never want to forget them. For them, they were hours of togetherness with their classmates and friends. I know, I know these hours too. But I didn't like many of these events. They weren't my games that were played there. I most certainly didn't want to play according to rules that were set and controlled by the pioneer leaders or teachers.

One of these unpopular events was the cops and robbers game. I had to sit still all afternoon, hiding behind a bush, until someone finally found me. I was very angry. I would have preferred to just go home. In the end, I couldn't be happy that I was one of the few people who hadn't been found. I wanted to play something else, something I enjoyed, not what I was supposed to.

Renate and Aunt Frieda

I had a cousin of the same age, Renate. Her mother was my father's older sister, whose first husband had died in the war. She married a second time. She had two daughters from her first marriage and her new husband had a son. Today we call that a patchwork family. So Renate had three different half-siblings. My last memory of her was my 10th birthday, the last children's birthday party she attended.

For reasons of space, we were both supposed to sleep together in one bed. That was very nice for us. I can't remember what was actually so funny in the books under the quilt. Maybe it was just the joy of the forbidden game with the flashlight, but you can only laugh with someone you like and understand. I

16

remember that we also sang songs to each other. Her favorite song was "Weiße Boote"[9]. She sang the chorus: "Weia candios"[10] so loudly, perhaps so terribly, that our parents came into the room and told us to be quiet. Otherwise they would have to separate us. But we didn't want that after all.

As children, we were important to each other. Today, we each lead our own lives. Nothing can simply be continued after such a long time. I still have postcards from her from the summer camp. She doesn't even remember that she was there, in Schöllerhau. "How are you? I'm doing well. Your Renate." She has lived in Munich since 1958 and, as far as I know, has never visited her homeland again.

Mr. Winkler

Today, after all these years, I know that the distinguished old Mr. Winkler was one of the people who made a deep impression on me in my childhood like no other. But he could not have foreseen that he would lay the foundation for my further development and my attitude to life.

At first, I didn't know what to make of him. The villagers were prejudiced against him. No one in the village knew anything about his past. He had moved here after the war. In those days, old people often sat on chairs or benches in front of their houses in the summer and talked to each other. Old Mr. Winkler never did that.

Was he too delicate? Perhaps he was. In any case, he stood out from the other villagers. The local men walked around in work clothes, Manchester pants with suspenders and checked shirts. Mr. Winkler always wore a plain shirt with a vest and a matching tie.

9 White Boats
10 Vaya con Dios

He didn't seem to fit in with the village at all. He seemed like a professor. They made fun of him. It was at the time when Walter Ulbricht was already waiting in the wings to replace Wilhelm Pieck. It was said that Winkler had sued someone who had called him a goatee. In fact, he also had a beard like Walter Ulbricht. Some said that he also had those cunning little eyes.

As soon as he approached a group of storytellers with his stick, everyone fell silent and Winkler passed them by like an ice-cold shiver.

The old-timers found it all the more surprising that the children suddenly took an interest in him and asked: "What have you to do with him?"

The children laughed and replied: "It's interesting with him" and ran off with all sorts of things under their arms.

Back then, I was one of the children who visited Mr. Winkler. The first time a younger playmate took me along. He had said: "Mr. Winkler can build great kites, which he then gives away. If you come along, he might give you one too." I don't remember why I went with him. At least not for the kite. It may have been curiosity, a thirst for adventure or a test of courage.

I remember my first visit when the old gentleman at the top of the stairs looked down over the banister and asked: "What kind of tall lady is Mr. Eckhard bringing with him today?"

That sounded funny and then again it didn't. He held out his hand with the signet ring. I could see that his fingernails were clean and well-groomed. His father's hands, on the other hand, were two big paws and never had spotlessly clean fingernails.

I was overwhelmed by what I found here. On a round table were lots of sticker-covered screw-top jars with thick absorbent cotton cocoons, brown manikins, caterpillars and butterflies. Suddenly, I was engrossed in an interesting conversation with the old man. He showed me a jar containing a green caterpillar about 5 cm long with black horizontal stripes and red dots all over its body. I had always been disgusted by the small green caterpillars that hung from apple trees on long threads. But this caterpillar here looked very pretty. It was sitting on a carrot leaf and it was funny to watch the appetite with which it nibbled on it. *Papilio Machaon Linne* was written on the glass. "What kind of butterfly do you think it will grow into?" asked Mr. Winkler. We children had no idea and tried unsuccessfully to guess which butterfly the beautiful caterpillar might one day become.

In one corner of the hallway stood an octagonal cupboard made of fly screen. In it, various species of butterfly fluttered around a tree-like green plant or sat on small bowls of fruit or liquid, sipping them.

The old man saved us: "That's the one there," he said, pointing to a beautiful yellow butterfly with a black border and two red dots on its pointed hind wings. "It's called a swallowtail in German and is the largest and most beautiful butterfly in our area."

He also gave the names of the other butterflies: Red Admiral, Apollo, Painted Lady, Blue, Large Tortoiseshell, Silver-washed Fritillary or Peacock.

Then he showed me and the other children even larger colorful butterflies, which were in numerous display cases. The largest butterflies came from South Africa and Brazil. Some were almost as big as a bat.

When I talked to the old man, I suddenly had the feeling that he was getting younger and looked less stern.

On many afternoons, I went through the meadows with other children and collected caterpillars, chrysalises, beetles and butterflies in empty jam jars for Mr. Winkler. We always took a piece of the plant on which we had found the insects. That's what Mr. Winkler had told us. When we came back, we wouldn't let him rest until he showed us which butterfly the caterpillar we had found would become or what the little beetle was called. He usually knew the answer off the top of his head.

I soon stopped finding the old man strange. You could learn a lot from him. He had numerous identification books, a microscope, magnifying glasses and tweezers. He had insecticides for killing insects, which he wouldn't let children touch, and means to prevent the beautiful colors of the wings from fading. He showed the children how to prepare a butterfly for the collection box. He gently placed the body between two small boards and carefully inserted a very thin special needle through the breastplate.

It was an interesting time. But when I was in eighth grade, I stopped going to him. Although I passed his house every day on my way to school, it soon seemed strange to me to still visit him as a big girl. Now there were other younger children at the old man's house.

My brother and the town

When I was nine, my brother, who had trained as a butcher, moved out of my parents' house and lived in Aschersleben with a girlfriend, whom he later married. Christa was like a big sister to me. After he met her, I got on much better with him too.

I loved it in the city. It was different from the village. There were cinemas, a museum, a swimming pool, a gondola pond and lots of bookshops. Christa even had a television and my brother had an EMW motorbike with a sidecar.

Once during the vacations, Hans and Christa went camping for a few days with a couple they were friends with at the Bremer Teich and took me with them in the sidecar. That was the best time I ever had with them. We swam around the lake, picked blueberries and mushrooms and lived like hunter-gatherers. Once we went out at night in rubber boots through a shallow tributary of the lake and, armed with forks and flashlights, searched for crabs. We used the forks to catch the crabs and collected them in a bucket of water. The next day, we threw the gray crabs into boiling water and they turned completely red. I felt sorry for the crabs, but I did what everyone else did, cracked open the crab legs and ate the white meat, which tasted delicious.

When I was 12 years old, I became the aunt of a boy. I slowly outgrew my childhood. I loved taking the baby for walks and had a lot of fun watching the little one learn to talk. The fact that he said Haubschruber instead of Hubschrauber[11] and called me Isesa was funny, childish words that have been memorized. At first, they were probably filed in the brain under laughable things. Today, everything is linked to the thought: it's a shame that everything turned out differently.

Nothing has turned out the way it would have if they hadn't left.

I always associate songs with loved ones. They have remained firmly in my memory. *„Sindi, oh Sindi, dein Herz muss traurig sein, der Mann, den du geliebt, ließ dich allein."*[12] Christa's favorite song, it will become a melody of destiny. I

---

11 helicopter
12 Sindi, oh Sindi, your heart must be sad, the man you loved left you alone.

will play it on my mandolin for many years to come and search for the sadness, as if I could use it to find something lost.

In April 1961, my brother and his family fled to the West. It was a Sunday. When I woke up in the morning, everything was different in our apartment. There were boxes and suitcases on the floor, my brother's TV on the sideboard and a birdcage with Jumbo the budgie in the window.

My parents had fetched these things from my brother's apartment on foot in the night using a handcart over the 10 km country road.

They were exhausted and excited. People from the police or state security would certainly come soon to find out about Hans and his family's escape and to check whether my parents and I had anything to do with it. We had to come up with a credible story.

"They usually come to the children first, because they're the easiest to blab," the father had said.

They couldn't help but let me in on it. I was told to say that I didn't know anything and I wasn't allowed to talk to anyone about it. But now that I did know something, I had to be able to lie convincingly. And this time it wasn't just a white lie. "Look me in the eye," my father had often demanded when he wasn't sure whether I was telling the truth. "Lies have short legs. It all comes out anyway."

I practiced for hours in front of the mirror and kept checking the effect on others, correcting my facial expressions and the tone of my words until I was sure I was delivering it correctly. It wasn't easy to look someone firmly in the eye and lie. Eyes were not allowed to blink or swerve, let alone look down in shame, that was suspicious.

In their lives, my parents had learned that you cannot rebel against dictatorships. But they were still able to live in harmony with their conscience.

My mother said: "Always remember the song *Die Gedanken sind frei*[13]. Who can guess them? It will help you and give you strength. If you feel that what you should do is wrong, you must not do it, but look for ways out. There is always a good solution."

My father told me that there had been a riot in the mine in 1953 and the ringleaders were to be arrested. He had helped one of them to escape by driving him out of the mine in his electric locomotive. The man wasn't a criminal, he had just campaigned for better working conditions. He had fled to the West with his family that very night. The police had waited in vain for him at the wrong end of the mine. He looked at me seriously and added: "Never join a party. If it all changes, they'll hold you responsible!"

I had been looking forward to living in the city with my brother and his family soon. That was over now. But I would never betray them in my life. My parents could rely on me.

First contact with state security

In fact, two men in long coats came the next day. It was a month before my 14th birthday. My parents had just left for the lunch shift and I was playing ball with the neighborhood kids in the yard. The men matched the description my parents had given me. They questioned me for quite a while, but I was well prepared and knew exactly what to say: "My brother doesn't live here anymore. He's married and lives in the city. I don't know where he is. I haven't seen him for a long time, I think four weeks."

---

13 The thoughts are free.

The men seemed to have been convinced by my statements and the innocent, unsuspecting look. They smiled and left. The ones with the long coats couldn't make an impression on me, no matter how friendly they pretended to be.

Nevertheless, this interrogation was a first incisive experience. Not everyone could be trusted. You had to think carefully about what and who you were allowed to tell.

The carefree, happy child I had been, who could get on with anyone, soon became a withdrawn, thoughtful teenager. I never told anyone about my brother and his family.

Chapter II – My youth

My youth was a very thoughtful and withdrawn time. I think the loss of loved ones affected me and left their mark on me. Sometimes I missed them very much and I had to think: "It's as if they've died. But it's actually much worse. They are alive and I don't know where. I can no longer reach them." They became missing persons in a war that takes place in the soul. Relatives, confidants, friends or enemies of the state? I started writing poems and diaries. Almost all of them were lost, because in the end I was one of those who left and couldn't take anything with me. A poem about the disintegration of our family is still in my head today, a poem that you couldn't recite, you had to hide it. It was important to me. I could use it to protest and mourn. But I won't write it down again. I don't want anyone to think I thought the bumpy verses were poetry. I will continue to carry it inside me.

I don't think I've become a sad or resentful person. What I've mentioned so far could give you the impression that I have. If anything, I've always tried to process, explain and under-stand everything. Of course, I also got to know the silly or happy sides of youth. But a lot of things were superficial and I didn't make any real friends in my youth, like I did as a child. It was often easiest to withdraw. I created my own world. Fantasy became more important to me than reality.

Berlin shortly before the Wall was built in 1961

The history teacher, Mr. Eggers, had organized a final trip to Berlin for the eighth graders. His easy-going, funny manner was well received by the pupils. Nevertheless, I was not one of those who revealed myself to him.

We went to the Brandenburg Gate, which was still open at the time. Only a few border guards checked our IDs. The teacher spoke briefly to one of the uniformed men and then said with a wink: "Come on, kids! We're all off to the West now, but of course we'll be back." It was meant to be funny, but it was also macabre. While the others in the class followed the teacher laughing, I had my own sad thoughts. I imagined that the brother and sister-in-law with the baby in the baby carriage had left here through this gate forever a few months earlier.

In preparation for the school trip, we had watched a movie about the Reichstag fire in 1933. A particularly tragic role was played by a young man from Holland who was supposed to have set the fire. His name was Marinus van der Lubbe, he was 25 years old and politically left-wing. He did not speak German well enough and one had to get the impression that the Nazis only needed a scapegoat to take action against the communists. They used him to seize power. Lubbe was sentenced to death in Leipzig on January 10, 1934.

For a few minutes, I stood with my classmates in front of the old Reichstag building, which was left over from Hitler's time. The once magnificent palace looked sooty and ready for demolition. The dome had collapsed and the window panes were broken. It was a ruin from the time when there had still been a single Germany. Now there were two German states.

There was no question for us pupils that the GDR was the better German country. It was only logical that socialism would one day triumph all over the world. That's how I put it in my last civics assignment and got a good grade.

13.08.1961: Construction of the Berlin Wall

On the orders of the GDR government under Walter Ulbricht, armed forces began to seal off the borders to West Berlin with barbed wire on the night of August 12-13, 1961. On August 17 and 18, construction began on the so-called anti-fascist protective wall, the Berlin Wall, which was 156 kilometers long in total. Officially, this was to prevent the influence of fascists and militarists. In reality, however, something had to be done urgently to keep GDR citizens in the country. Too many people had already fled and there were bottlenecks in the economy. Now, in one fell swoop, 16 million people were prevented from running away.

My parents and I were very shocked when we heard about the border closures in Berlin on the news.

My mother suffered greatly from the departure of her son and grandchild and often cried. There was probably no chance of seeing her again soon.

My father said reproachfully: "You didn't want to go back then. Now it's too late."

20.08.1961: Vacation with my parents in the Harz Mountains

For the first and only time in their lives, my parents treated themselves to a vacation in the Harz Mountains together with a couple they were friends with. They thought I couldn't be sent to a children's holiday camp at the age of 14. After all, I had already had my Jugendweihe[14] and was taller than my mother. I looked almost grown-up with my tousled hairdo and, like all the other teenagers, I was now wearing mini-skirts and heels, much to the chagrin of my mother, who

---

14 Jugendweihe ("Youth consecration") or Jugendfeier ("Youth ceremony") is a secular coming of age ceremony for German 14-year-olds.

could no longer sew frilly children's dresses, and to the chagrin of my father, who noticed how the young men were looking at me. I would have preferred not to go away with my parents at all, because then I would have had to subordinate myself like a toddler. I had other ideas about going on vacation, I would have preferred to stay at home and do something with my friends, like swimming, dancing or going to the cinema. But I absolutely had to go with them so that I was under control. In the past, they hadn't been so strict about control either.

My parents had opted for accommodation in Elbingerode because they didn't need a pass here as they did in Elend or Schierke. Before the war, as young people, they had once climbed the Brocken[15] from Schierke. A weather station had been built there in 1939, which can still be seen from afar today. However, it had not been possible to climb the Brocken since the GDR was founded. Only meteorologists, who continued to collect climate data here and had to walk up from Schierke every day, were allowed to climb it.

The 1,142 m high mountain was located in the border area of the GDR and the Brocken plateau had become Soviet military territory after the war. Moscow's most westerly eavesdropping service was now setting up here, while the Americans and their eavesdropping services were located on the smaller Wurmberg opposite.

In between lay the inner-German border. It was mined and guarded by the GDR with dangerous shepherd dogs that moved around on leashes, barked loudly and would tear anyone who tried to escape to pieces.

---

15 The Brocken, also sometimes referred to as the Blocksberg, is a
   3,743 ft mountain near Schierke in the Saxony-Anhalt,
   between the rivers Weser and Elbe.

I wasn't sure whether my parents really only intended to spend their vacation here or whether they also wanted to gain an impression of the escape possibilities in the Harz Mountains.

In any case, escaping in this area would have been just as pointless as in Berlin, through which the death zone with the Wall now ran. Since my parents had bought a portable radio, I also got the chance to listen to music and news.

On August 24, the American radio station RIAS reported on the first Wall fatality, 24-year-old Günter Litfin. He was shot while swimming through the Humboldt harbour.

I wandered through the woods with my parents and their friends, along the Holtemme and the Steinerne Renne gorge, always a little way behind them, with the portable radio in my hand, and somehow went on my own vacation. They only left me alone because they were probably considerate of my adolescent age.

However, I had to admit that the landscape along the river was very impressive. At one point, we all sat down on the large round stones in the river. Then we heard a cuckoo in the distance.

As a small child, I used to call out: "Dear cuckoo, tell me how many more years I'll live!" Then I counted the cuckoo calls and rejoiced when there were many and I would be very old. I didn't shout the words now, but I still counted in silence. The cuckoo had stamina. He gave me another 40 years. Then it would be 2001. An unimaginable number of years. I would then be 54 years old. My mother would be 80 and my father 85. Well, it was all just incredible fun.

On another day, we climbed the Ottofelsen, a 36-metre-high boulder, using steep iron ladders and had a wonderful panoramic view. From here, the seemingly endless mountains of the Harz could not be seen to be divided into east and west. Behind us on a hill lay Wernigerode Castle and in front of us towered the massive, unreachable Brocken. We were only about 10 km from the German-German border as the crow flies. I thought I could hear the dogs guarding the border barking in the distance. But my father said: "You can't hear it that far away. You can't hear a dog barking in Aschersleben in Königsaue either!"

In Elbingerode, we met women in long black dresses and white hoods. "They are deaconesses," the mother explained, "Christian nuns who mainly work in nursing, in children's or old people's homes or in poor countries."

I found that very interesting. But I was quickly talked out of my enthusiasm for it. "Deaconesses are not allowed to marry and have children. I don't think you're cut out for that. You have to go back to school first."

Sept. 1961: At the EOS in the municipal town

Most of my childhood playmates went on to the 10-grade polytechnic secondary school in the village. My parents were proud that I was allowed to do my Abitur[16] at the EOS in the town. I still attended dance school for a few weeks in September 1961 with my former friends from home. But after that, contact became less and less frequent.

I had to take the local train to school every day and had to study a lot when I was at home.

Students from the surrounding villages and the city came to the Abitur class, usually two friends at a time. I was left behind and felt isolated. I wrote in my diary and tried to work through my problems and worries in poems and stories.

---

16 "A" Levels or GCSEs

I could lock the diary with a key that I wore on my necklace. At some point it got lost. But that's another story. I still remember some of those lost verses today.

The parents must have thought they were doing the best for their daughter. Little did they know that my time at EOS would be a very depressing time.

Shortly after joining the school, some teachers and students were expelled, allegedly for spreading anti-state views. Some students were about to take their Abitur exams. I didn't know them well, but when the English teacher, Mr. Giggel, who was very popular with everyone, said goodbye to the class forever by shaking everyone's hand and saying a few kind words, everyone's eyes filled with tears.

Later, a classmate from the parallel class committed suicide, allegedly out of lovesickness. Nobody close to her had any idea that something like that could happen. She was probably just as alone with her problems as I was. And if there hadn't been another unexpected event for me one day that finally brought help, who knows what would have happened to me.

1962: Farewell to Mr. Winkler

One day, as I was walking home from school, Mr. Winkler was standing outside the front door leaning on his cane. He looked pale and ill. I felt sorry for him and was very sorry that I hadn't contacted him for a long time. I wondered whether I should speak to him, but he took the first step towards me and said:

"I've been waiting for you. I've heard that you're learning English at school now." It really bothered me that he was

31

now addressing me as "Sie"[17]. It was as if we had become strangers again. "Please speak to me like you used to, Mr. Winkler, you make me feel strange."

"All right, but in the meantime, I'm looking at a young lady who had a youth consecration some time ago." A barely perceptible smile flitted across his face. He asked me to come up to his apartment because he wanted to show and tell me something important. This time it wasn't about the butterflies. He showed me letters and postcards from all over the world."

Only now did I learn that Mr. Winkler had been an interpreter and translator in his professional life. He spoke perfect Spanish, French and English. When he had to retire, he started collecting butterflies. He enjoyed it so much that he advertised in many foreign newspapers and contacted people from all over the world to exchange butterflies.

He asked me in a strangely touching way: "Do you think anyone would want to correspond with an octogenarian?" Then he told me that unfortunately he could only communicate with young people and he had to be young himself. So he saw no other option than to deceive his writing friends all over the world. He sent them photos from his youth and pretended to be a traveling salesman. He was actually an honest and honorable person. Now he wanted to clear his conscience and ask for forgiveness.

One pen friend was particularly close to his heart. He showed me a picture of a young Nigerian in the traditional dress of his Ibo tribe and said: "His name is Ibrahim Mamuru, he is an honest man and is not worth being lied to. I hope he can forgive me. Would you be interested in writing him the truth about me?"

---

17 The pokite form of address, as opposed to the familiar "Du".

32

I promised him I would.

When I asked him how he had got so many foreign addresses, Mr. Winkler wrote down the address of the organization *International Pen Friends* in Czechoslovakia.

Mr. Winkler actually died a few days later.

Ibrahim, my pen friend

I kept my promise and wrote the young man from Nigeria the truth about Mr. Winkler. Ibrahim then became my life-long pen friend. For him, Mr. Winkler had always been a young, open-minded man. He had never doubted that he was corresponding with a 25-year-old man.

I was 15 when the correspondence began. Ibrahim was six years older and already had some life experience. He became my living diary, to whom I could confide everything. He wrote reliably and always gave interesting answers to my questions. As I had to write the letters in English, I was soon better at English than the others in my class and gained insights that I would never have gained without him. Once I wrote to him about the divided Berlin and that the people in the GDR were imprisoned. They could never travel to a western country in their lives, even if they had the money. They were not free. He replied: "I'm not free either. I could travel wherever I wanted, but I don't have any money."

We realized that freedom was not for everyone and that we were among those who were disadvantaged because of our birth and would probably never be free.

At school, I learned in civics that freedom is an understanding of necessity. Should I realize that under socialism there could be no friends behind the borders? Wouldn't it be better to say: freedom is absolutely necessary?

My brother, who had been living in the West for a few years

now, would occasionally send a postcard from his vacation: from Tyrol, Lake Garda or Yugoslavia. I was thrilled by the beautiful, colorful cards and started to build up a collection of postcards. It was a nice hobby, but also a sad one, because I would never be able to travel to my brother or to the places on the postcards. I didn't talk to anyone about these thoughts. I also didn't know anyone in the class who had relatives in the West or other contacts abroad.

The girl who had had so many playmates in her childhood became a loner. I began to doubt everything and question everything critically.

Only my diary or Ibrahim knew what I was doing. While my mother sent parcels to the West and we also received parcels from the West, I wrote letters. The letters to my brother were mostly superficial, about the weather, everyday life or about the budgie Jumbo, who they had left behind and who now lived with budgie Jacki.

Nevertheless, my life settled into a kind of equilibrium. Although I was no longer at the top of my class at secondary school, I took part more intensively in extracurricular activities such as the school choir and drawing circle. In my free time, I not only wrote letters to my brother and Ibrahim, but had also obtained addresses from all over the world via pen friends in Czechoslovakia: Jaswant Singh Tind from India, Toshio Terai from Japan, Günter Schwarzer from Italy, Gerard Degieux from France and Bridget Shreadgill from England. The Russian teacher had also distributed addresses and hoped that this would improve his students' grades. So I also wrote to Nadejda Boizowa in the Soviet Union. I was always busy with myself and the other unknown people. I learned a lot about my pen friends and life in other countries. But sadly I would never meet these people face to face in my life.

1963: Demolition of my home village

The government decided to demolish the village of Königsaue and relocate the inhabitants to the district town and to a new village to be built. Lignite coal was important for the national economy. First the graves in the cemetery were reburied. Then huge excavators and bulldozers ate their way through the village. All the buildings were blown up and reduced to rubble: the water tower, the Schoch manor house, which had become our school, the cultural center, the agricultural warehouse, the marjoram factory, the windmill, the two churches and, of course, the 15-family house where I had spent my childhood.

We were given a new apartment in the district town and no longer lived with our former neighbors.

Leaving the village was difficult for many people, especially the older ones. I had the advantage of already knowing Aschersleben. I had been going to school there for two years by train or bus and my brother had lived there before that time. But it was still very sad to see how the village was destroyed and lost forever. Places where I had played with friends and schoolmates only existed in memory. New Year's Eve 1962 will remain unforgettable. The vicar, Maria's father, had given us permission for Maria, Gudrun and I to ring the bells of the Protestant church. We worked hard, took turns hanging on the ropes and set the bells in motion to ring in the New Year. But it was a sad farewell. It was the first and last time I rang the bells. A short time later, the church where I was baptized, witnessed weddings and saw nativity plays at Christmas was blown up.

Like many other people, however, I had to get used to the fact that everything was changing. The never-ending farewells to loved ones were already part of everyday life. And now I had to say goodbye to the village and its people. There was no point in complaining about it together with other people. My contacts with my friends and classmates didn't break up for good, but we became more and more distant as everyone moved to a new place. Writing helped me to process things and became a necessary life aid. Where the former village of Königsaue was is now the Königsauer See[18]. Surrounded by bushes and trees, it is now an inaccessible nature reserve, a paradise for birds and rare animal species.

1965: Julia and the graduation trip to Hungary

As you go through life, there are always nice events that leave a lasting impression. The popular English teacher Dr. Blume had organized a German/Hungarian class exchange for the final trip of the Abitur class, with the intention of getting to know the country and its people and promoting the English language.

The class exchange to Hungary was exceptional by GDR standards. Normally, this kind of thing was only known from western countries, where people went to England or France to learn the local language.

Not all the parents in my class were able to raise the necessary money for the trip to Hungary. But my parents did every-thing they could to help me.

First Julia came to my German family, then I went to Julia. We both got on very well straight away. That was a good reason for me to learn some Hungarian, and Julia learned German. We kept on visiting each other, even when we later had our own families and children[19].

In the early years, we only spoke English with each other and

18 Lake
19 The contact between us still exists today.

always had to have our dictionaries with us. We needed a lot of imagination if we wanted to say something and didn't know the words.

I really liked Hungary. Everything was brighter and more colorful there than in the GDR. Through the close contact with Julia's family, I got to know more of the country than any other vacationer who only went to Lake Balaton or Budapest. I felt almost at home with Julia's family. Her parents and brother were very close to me and we always had a lot of fun together.

1965: Abitur and Bernd

I did what all young people did, went to the movies or dancing. I shared my hobbies of singing and drawing with a classmate. As we went to the same study groups, we gradually became friends. I got to know other young people from the city, fell in love and broke up again. None of the young men could hold a candle to my Nigerian pen friend. There had to be someone I could tell everything to and who would always stick by me.

My training was called Abitur with a skilled worker's certificate. You had to work on the estate for a week and you spent three weeks at school.

Once a month, I met up with other high school graduates at the Volksgut whose education was similar, except that they were called skilled workers with a high school diploma. One of them was Bernd, a good-looking, interesting student, the same age as me. He was very different from the others, could play the guitar and had a very special opinion of his own. He had grown up in a children's home. His parents had fled to the West when he was three years old, leaving him and two other siblings behind. Actually, he should have been grateful to the state that he had grown up in a children's home. But he had experienced a lot of bad things that he would probably never get over. He was not on good terms with the teachers. There was no end to the punishments in the home. How often did he have to stand barefoot in the corridor at night with his hands up just because he had whispered something to his bedmate? He caught a cold and fell ill. How often did he experience that he didn't even get a piece of chocolate at Christmas? The teachers had taken everything home for their own children. Nobody in the home cared about the children's souls. He never sat on anyone's lap, no one comforted him or checked his homework or helped him with problems. No, the ideology of the state was not the one he believed in. The fact that he made it into an A-level class at all was solely down to his strong will. Bernd was very intelligent and loved mathematics and biology. He was also a very good sportsman and won several prizes in the 100 m race. He already seemed like an adult. I admired him for what he had done with himself.

In the meantime, the last school year was coming to an end and the Abitur exams were coming up. I passed the Abitur with a satisfactory grade. I only got A grades in English and art education. My dream was to become a porcelain painter in Meissen, which unfortunately didn't work out. I applied for an apprenticeship in lithography and also as a glass painter. In the end, I ended up studying education, specializing in biology and chemistry, which was not my first choice.

I had now known Bernd for six months and we each had our own ideas about the future and our studies. In the next few months we would go our separate ways; I would go to Güstrow (Mecklenburg) to study education, he would go to Löbau (Saxony) to the officers' college. We would write to each other and see each other again from time to time. The distance between us would probably have led to our separation at some point.

But things turned out differently and it would have been better if they hadn't. I had only just started my studies when I realized that I was pregnant.

Chapter III – Study, children, work

1965/66: Marriage, left university. Frank's birth, divorce

I think we both saw it as our duty to get married. Bernd didn't want to bring a child into the world that would grow up without a father. He wanted to start a family that he hadn't had himself. But it wasn't going to be that easy, we were both only 18 and had just started our education. We each wanted to finish our studies.

We got married on December 31, 1965, surrounded only by my parents and grandparents. A dream wedding looked different.

Our son Frank was born shortly before the exams at the teacher training college. I had to give up my studies because I wouldn't have passed the exams. I had neither the time to study nor the courage and strength to believe in myself. Bernd was not the loving partner I had wished for, he was still too young and inexperienced to be a good father and husband. It was like two children having one child. We still lived with my parents in half a room. There were often arguments. Bernd couldn't play the guitar because it disturbed the others, especially the baby. I couldn't write any letters or diaries because Bernd would have been jealous. I was happy when he went back to Löbau.

I attended a course in shorthand and typing at the adult education center. After that, I took a job as a typist in the housing construction combine. Once I had to help out in the canteen, peeling potatoes, because people were missing. I happened to overhear people talking about me: "She can't even peel potatoes."

"No wonder! She has A-levels."

"She was always a spoiled child. When it came to selecting

her for A-levels, the school chose her instead of a boy who had the same grades, just because she was a working-class child and his parents were self-employed. She should have done without the Abitur place, because in the end she didn't get anywhere."

It hurt to hear that. My fellow human beings thought nothing of me. They looked me in the face and talked condescendingly behind my back. I tried not to let it affect me. But I realized myself that I couldn't do that. I had actually failed.

After a year and a half of working as a typist in housing construction, I finally broke up with Bernd.

He had found my diary and the letters from Ibrahim and read them. Afterwards, he called me stupid and naive. When I started to cry, he took the diary and the letters and tore them up in front of me. For me, they were the most important records that had given me stability in life. For him, it was just children's stuff.

When I said to him: "I'm going to get a divorce", he just replied: "Do it!"

He drove back to Löbau and I filed for divorce the very next day. We got divorced quickly and without any problems because we agreed that we weren't compatible. I was just 20 and got custody. But it was actually my mother who lovingly looked after her grandson until he was 5 years old. She had given up her job in mining and I worked full-time in the office instead.

Once at the weekend, Bernd picked up his little son and did something with him. I held back, but my parents told him it would be better if he stopped coming. "The child will only be torn back and forth."

He stopped coming and my son never got to know his father. I wasn't happy with my situation. I regretted that I hadn't at least tried to continue my studies. My salary as a typist was too low and my self-esteem was "in the basement". I had failed even before my adult life had begun.

1967/1968: Halle-Neustadt

When the company suggested that I go to Halle-Neustadt to work in assembly in order to earn more, I accepted the offer in consultation with my parents. At that time, numerous pre-fabricated apartments were being built in Halle-Neustadt for the chemical workers at Leuna and Buna.

I was housed in a workers' hostel during the week, like everyone else who was on assembly. I became friends with Vera, a single woman of the same age. We both worked as typists in the technical department, which included various construction engineers.

Apart from the department manager, we were all young and adventurous people. We often arranged to meet up after work to do something together and soon became a close-knit community.

Strangely enough, the things I remember most about Halle-Neustadt were my experiences with the People's Police. One evening was pretty idiotic when the whole group wanted to go to the Steintor Varieté in Halle.

We were running late and it had become dark in the meantime. We had to cross the road not far from a streetcar stop. As the traffic lights had a very long red phase and no cars were coming, we quickly crossed the road in single file. But two policemen were already waiting at the other end. One after the other we were ticketed and had to pay a fine of 15 marks.

Another time, we had organized a social get-together in our offices after work. There had been plenty of alcohol and we danced into the night. At midnight on the dot, three police officers came to break up the party because it hadn't been registered. "Please leave the building immediately and go home!"

The secretary, a well-proportioned thirty-year-old with long red hair, had worked up enough courage and tried to be charming: "But dear policemen, don't be like that."

Two of the policemen tried to push her out. She shouted: "Don't touch me, you bastards!" She lashed out and slapped one of them hard across the face, her fingernails leaving a trail of blood on his face. She broke away and ran off. It was clear to everyone that there would be repercussions.

The next day, the secretary had gone to the hairdresser before starting work and came to work with a short blonde hairstyle.

Around noon, the three police officers returned to the shack to find the redhead. The work colleagues were happy to provide information, but no one knew a woman who matched the police description, not even the blonde, short-haired secretary, who otherwise knew everything.

Almost everyone had a portable radio with them early in the morning when they went to work on the street between the large blocks of flats at around 6.00 am. The police in Halle-Neustadt ensured peace and order and were always around to catch troublemakers. But youth wouldn't be youth if it didn't provoke. Even I allowed myself to join in. We turned the portable radios up loud and walked down the street, at the end of which the police were already waiting for us. When we got closer, we turned off the music. Of course, we were checked and threatened to pay a fine or they would confiscate the radios. Each time, we claimed that we hadn't turned our radios on, it must have been someone else. And it's not illegal to take a radio to work, is it?

The government was particularly proud of Block 10, which at 380 m was the longest residential block in the GDR. On 10 floors, in which there were 536 one-room and 320 multi-room apartments, 3000 people could live. That was 1000 more than had lived in my village.

Once, in March 1968, I experienced Walter Ulbricht's visit here, which was a strange event for me.

I was standing just a few meters behind a barrier in front of the Chairman of the State Council and had a good look at him. I was startled for a moment. His face looked yellowish, like a wax doll, without any facial expressions, as if he wasn't a living person. He gave a speech of thanks to the construction workers and spoke about the further development of socialism in the chemical workers' town. It wasn't just about building schools, crèches, kindergartens and shopping centers, but also about improving cultural life.

It was one of those speeches that you heard again and again. I could feel neither enthusiasm nor rejection, just emptiness and helplessness, and my mind wandered. When I was 15, I used to secretly listen to Radio Luxembourg and the latest Beatles hits at night. I had corresponded with Ibrahim about it and learned English with enthusiasm. Walter Ulbricht had publicly embarrassed himself with his statement on beat music when he said: „*Ist es denn wirklich so, dass wir jeden Dreck, der vom Westen kommt, nur kopieren müssen? Ich denke, Genossen, mit der Monotonie des Je-Je-Je, und wie das alles heißt, ja, sollte man doch Schluss machen.*"[20]

I remember nothing of Ulbricht's speech to the construction

---

20 *Is it really the case that we just have to copy every piece of filth that comes from the West? I think, comrades, we should put an end to the monotony of Je-Je-Je and whatever it's all called.*

workers. But I can still see that yellowish wax face in front of me today.

In Halle Neustadt there were various stores in the shopping street, such as a department store, post office and pharmacy, but there was also a small restaurant with a jukebox. You could press a button and pay a fee to listen to records there. We went there several times after work, had a drink and listened to music. Once, however, we overdid it. The men liked Hazy Osterwald's "Criminal Tango" and played it several times. They asked us women to dance. But the landlord wouldn't allow it: "This is not a dance hall. Leave the restaurant immediately, otherwise I'll have to call the police!"

It was a beautiful summer evening and far too early to go to bed. So we decided to go swimming at the quarry pond and listen to music from the portable radio. We couldn't dance the tango to pop music by Frank Schöbel and Chris Doerk, but the men jumped off the cliffs of the quarry pond and dived into the water to the tune of "Links von mir, rechts von mir".

Whe[21]n there were no dates with my work colleagues, I would spend the evenings reading the textbooks I still had from my aborted biology/chemistry degree. I knew that assembly time was a temporary thing. It couldn't go on like this for the rest of my life.

Many of my work colleagues were married or had families and were going home for the weekend. Vera was also getting married soon. Everything would change. I had had a good time in Halle Neustadt, but I had to think about the future and be there for my little son. A new phase in my life had to begin.

---

21 To the left of me, to the right of me

When the time came for the entrance exams at the Pädagogisches Institute in Kröllwitz, I got all the documents I needed to study again and reapplied for the biology/chemistry course. Above all, I wanted to prove to myself that I could complete this course. I passed the entrance exam, but I was told emphatically that I was costing the state money and that if I dropped out of this course again, I would never get a place again.

August 1968: Hungary, Puszta, Flower carnival Debrecen
Before I started studying again, I went to Hungary to visit Julia for two weeks. It was my second visit after the class exchange. Julia was now studying foreign trade in Budapest and had a semester break, just like her brother, who was studying in Moscow. So we were able to spend time together. Julia's brother was now fluent in Russian. Our general language of communication, however, remained English. Julia's parents enjoyed giving us a good time. They weren't rich, but they weren't poor either. Her father was a master bricklayer and his own boss, her mother was a housewife with heart and soul. She cooked and baked the tastiest cakes and dishes in the small bakery on the farm. We often had breakfast outside at the table under the big chestnut tree. Father was the type of Hungarian you would imagine, tanned, with a moustache and always in a good mood. He always made a ceremony out of breakfast. He came to the table with a bottle of Barack Palinka and shot glasses the size of 2 cl and insisted on drinking a glass first. I wasn't used to drinking alcohol, but for the sake of hospitality I couldn't refuse and put up with it.
Once it got quite embarrassing for me, and not just because I was tipsy. Julia's father raised his glass: "Egészségedre! Cheers!" When I returned the toast, everyone started laughing

and didn't want to stop. Julia explained why: "You must pronounce the word long, like: egges scheegedre. If you say schegg, that's a bad word. She pointed to her backside. Aha, I had understood. "Bocsánat. Sorry." Afterwards we had a little black coffee (kis fekete kávé) and then freshly baked kifli[22] with apricot jam and melon.

There were also misunderstandings at lunch.

My stomach rejected some of the unfamiliar dishes, such as lecho or chicken soup with chicken legs that still had their claws on. For Julia's father, however, it was a delicacy. He liked to take my chicken leg and nibble the skin off it with relish. I had a really bad time with the spicy fish soup. After the first spoonful, I had to gasp for air so much that I feared I would choke. As a kind of resuscitation a clap on my back meant that everything went well again.

Julia and I had experienced something similar the year before with her brother, who couldn't keep the tartare (raw minced beef with egg, onions and spices) that was popular in the GDR. Since then, we used the word tartare for everything we didn't like. It was perfectly acceptable to refuse something before it got worse. The hosts came to realize that as a foreigner you couldn't tolerate everything. Other peoples, other customs. So it went far beyond hospitality.

---

22 A traditional yeast bread roll that is rolled and formed into a crescent before baking, a common type of bread roll throughout much of central Europe and nearby countries, where it is called by different names and is thought to be the inspiration for the French *croissant*.

Puszta

Once Julia, her brother József and I went with their father to the Puszta, to Hortobagy to the bridge market, near the famous Nine-Arch Bridge. It wasn't far from Debrecen. At some point, their father turned off the country road onto a dirt road that led through a poor settlement consisting of just a few small mud houses with thatched roofs. Chickens, geese and pigs ran along the village road and in between them, little snotty-nosed children ran around in dirty, torn clothes. Julia's father had to drive very slowly and watch out like hell to make sure nothing happened. Women in long, colorful dresses sat in front of the houses and talked to each other as if this was the most normal thing in the world. Some of them had bared their breasts and were breastfeeding their babies.

I had never seen poverty in Hungary before and felt sorry for these people. This was a complete contrast to life in Julia's family or my own. It was the dark side of life and we lived on the sunny side.

But Julia explained to me that I didn't need to feel sorry for them. They were Sinti and Roma and it was their free will to live like this.

The state had probably tried to accommodate them in new buildings and get them used to regular work, but this only succeeded witha small number of them. Many did not want a different life. What they were excellent at, however, was playing the violin and other string instruments.

Behind the settlement stretched a seemingly endless yellow-green steppe land with a huge sky above it, the vast lowlands of the Puszta. Every now and then an old farm could be seen in the landscape or an old draw well stretching its arms far into the air. We observed how skillfully the shepherds rode their horses and gave orders to the dogs to keep the herds of sheep or horses together. Particularly impressive were the herds of gray cattle with their mighty curved pointed horns, which you don't see anywhere else.

A small festival was held at a csárda not far from the Nine-Arch Bridge. Dark-clad horsemen put on a unique show for the guests. Standing on two horses at the same time, they drove two other horses in front of them or
encouraged them to stand on two legs, sit down or lie down. "Perhaps they are Attila's descendants who settled here after the Mongol invasions," Julia's father tried to explain. On an open-air stage, musicians played beautiful melodies on their violins and a group of young women and men in folk costumes danced to them. (Ritka búza, ritka àrpa, ritka rozs) An ox was roasted on a spit and kettle goulash was served.

Numerous vendors offered their wares: Paprika and garlic braids, tomatoes, melons, apricots; basketry, tablecloths. I bought a red leather-covered shepherd's flask for my father, a wicker basket for my mother and a wooden horse for my little son.

Carnival of Flowers

It was August 20, 1968, National Day in Hungary and the last day before my departure. Julia, József and I went to see the flower carnival in Debrecen, the largest flower festival in Europe, which was part of the festivities. The float parade was led by the float with the replica of the Hungarian crown. It consisted of a shiny golden flower arrangement with red flower inlays and a golden cross on top. Many floats with different floral compositions and singing and celebrating people joined and drove through the city center. We stood at the side of the road with many other people and watched the colorful spectacle. It was loud in the city. Bands were playing the songs of the band Omega, whose lead singer, the blond, long-haired János Kóbor, was Julia's favorite. She called him Mecky. For me, he was something like a Hungarian Beatle. In the crowd, we bumped into Arpad and Marika, who had also taken part in the student exchange. We danced and partied with them and the many other people on the streets until late in the evening.

My bag was packed. It was time to go to bed. I was going home tomorrow. I was looking forward to seeing my little son and his parents again. I had had a great time with Julia and her brother and had recovered well. We had often gone swimming, mostly in the Debrecen baths, which they called the beach. We had great fun in the wave pools. Once we even went to the cave baths in Hajduszoboszlo with Julia's father. We swam through the cave passages, sat under a waterfall and let the water run over our heads.

I fell asleep contentedly. In the middle of the night, however, there was suddenly a deafening bang over the house. I jumped out of bed in shock. All I could hear was a roar that got quieter and quieter. But then everything repeated itself. A terrible noise came closer, got louder and louder and it banged over the house. I didn't know what to think. Had a war started? I assumed it was low-flying airplanes flying over the house at short intervals. They were coming from the east.

Julia, who was sleeping in the next room, was just as worried and turned on the radio. "There is unrest in Czechoslovakia, in Prague", she said, "counter-revolution and Dubcek". Was there going to be a repeat of what happened in the GDR in 1953 and in Hungary in 1956?

"How am I supposed to get home now?" I asked. Julia shrugged her shoulders.

The Hungarian news announced in the morning that a special train was being set up for all GDR vacationers in Budapest, which was returning via the Ukraine and Poland. We didn't find out exactly what was going on in Czechoslovakia. But we could assume that the armies of the socialist states would intervene. The Soviet Union under Leonid Brezhnev had overall control of all socialist countries and no deviation from the course would be allowed. Dubcek's reforms for a more humane socialism in Czechoslovakia had to be strictly prevented.

Julia and I hadn't given much thought to politics before. We lived in our own world, which was all about studying and having fun. As a young mother, I already had more responsibility than she did, but my parents took a lot of it off my hands. Julia and I were by no means mature enough in our thoughts and actions.

Now we realized how much our future could depend on the actions of governments. Our whole lives could suddenly change.

21.08.1968: Special train to GDR (via Ukraine/Poland)

It had been announced that the special train from Budapest would also stop in Debrecen. Julia's mother gave me a large packed lunch and two bottles of water and hugged me. "Get home safely!"

Julia and her father took me to the station: "Let me know when you get home!" I had an uneasy feeling when we said goodbye to each other and I got on the train. Hopefully everything would go well.

The train was full of vacationers, many with schoolchildren or small children. Normally a journey from Budapest to Berlin would take about 15 hours. Now you had to reckon with

51

double that time, maybe even longer. After all, it was a journey into the unknown.

A young couple sat opposite me. I kept nodding off because I'd been up all night and hardly noticed the landscape we were driving through. After about three to four hours had passed, the journey ended at the Hungarian border station of Zahony, where there were railroad switches. Everyone had to get on another train, as only broad-gauge trains ran in the Ukraine and throughout the Soviet Union.

From Zahony onwards, the carriages were equipped with light-colored wooden benches and were not very comfortable. The train crossed the Tisza on a railroad bridge and soon reached the first Ukrainian station in Chop. Now the journey would take forever through the Ukraine. Sitting opposite me were young parents with a baby. They took turns looking after the little one, cradling it in their arms, giving it a bottle to suck on, feeding it porridge from a jar, diapering it and seeing no other option than to throw the smelly diapers out of the window. They were Pampers that they had probably received from West German relatives, because in the GDR and Hungary you couldn't buy these things yet.

The train passed through deserted areas and seemingly endless forests without stopping. Every now and then, huge fields appeared. Only once did I discover a small forest settlement and saw a woman in rubber boots and a thick gray cotton jacket walking along a soggy dirt road.

The train had probably also passed through towns or industrial areas. We must have passed through Lviv. But all I could remember was the enormous size of the country, the never-ending forests and the deserted areas. Somehow it was no longer a vacation trip. I just wanted to get home to my child and my parents.

The train stopped in Warsaw sometime around midnight. The night was dark and you couldn't see anything of the city from the station. I couldn't remember where the carriages with the hard wooden benches were changed. Anyway, we arrived in Görlitz on a train with leatherette benches, after about 40 hours since the train left Budapest. At the station, we were welcomed by volunteers and helpers from the German Red Cross, who handed out drinks and sandwiches and mainly looked after old people and mothers with children. I still had to catch a few connecting trains and was able to hold my parents and my little son in my arms again in the evening. Luckily everything had gone well, it would have been unthinkable if we had been separated forever.

Prague Spring

My parents and I learned what actually happened in Prague on the night of August 21, 1968 on West German television.

Half a million soldiers from the Soviet Union, Poland, Hungary and Bulgaria had marched into Czechoslovakia and occupied strategic points in the country. Soviet tanks were driving through Prague. There were deaths and injuries. Dubček, the 1st Secretary of the Communist Party and other high-ranking members of the government were arrested and taken to Moscow. There they were put under pressure and later gradually disempowered in favor of Gustáv Husák, who was loyal to the party line.

In a radio address, the President of Czechoslovakia, Ludvik Svoboda, called on his countrymen to remain calm. NATO kept quiet so as not to give the Soviet Union an excuse to intervene.

The so-called Prague Spring was over just two days later. But tens of thousands of Czechs and Slovaks left the country for Austria and West Germany to escape the expected reprisals.

1968-1972: Halle/Saale, study of pedagogy

I took my studies seriously, I owed it to my parents,
my child and myself. I lived at boarding school for another
two years with students who were younger than me, and of
course none of them were mothers yet. I went home at the
weekend. During the week, I waited tables after lectures in
pubs and ice cream parlors to support my parents financially.
My mother now worked by the hour as a kitchen assistant in
the kindergarten, where she could take Frank with her.

I got to know Michael when I was waitressing at the Haus
der Armee, a restaurant that was frequented by many members of the army. He was stationed in Halle and, as the cultural officer of his unit, even had his own office on the second
floor of the restaurant and his own apartment in another
street. He was divorced and had a 5-year-old son, whom he
often visited in the city. He made me an offer that I should do
some paperwork for him for a fee. I accepted the offer and
we became closer.

Michael was a very special person. He worked as a freelance
journalist. His parents were both practicing doctors and psy-
chiatrists. His sister lived in Switzerland. He knew the art
scene in Halle and was friends with the painter Harald
Döring, to whose studio he once took me. I had won a prize
for painting in the student competition, but perhaps a few
hours of painting with Döring could raise my level a little. In
the end, nothing came of it. I had to earn money and I went
home at the weekend. Michael went with me a few times and
originally had serious intentions. He took my oil painting
"Mother and Child" with him to have it framed.

Once we went to visit his parents. The visit was a shocking
experience for me. At the door, the mother greeted her son
not with a hug, but with reproachful words to the effect that

he must have known that the appointment was inappropriate because neither the cook nor the cleaning lady were there. I would have liked to leave on the spot. But then she forced us into the house after all. I felt very uncomfortable as an uninvited guest, but also because I had never been in such a stately home before. I could only compare everything to my simple life and was overwhelmed by the abundance of treasures. In the spacious drawing room, there was a large floor vase decorated with gold trim and the most beautiful flowers, which would have cost an office worker a month's wages. Designers had probably decorated the whole house. The carpets and curtains, the blankets and cushions on the sofas, everything was color-coordinated. The walls were hung with original paintings that were probably by famous artists and would have fetched large sums of money if they had been sold. Everything was exquisite and special. There was beautifully designed Scandinavian furniture that you couldn't buy in any department store in the GDR. There were precious illustrated books in the bookcases, Meissen porcelain figurines in the glass cabinets and silver candlesticks on the piano. Many of these things had supposedly been left to them by patients who had no descendants. Michael's mother called a restaurant and had some food delivered. She took the chicken pieces to the kitchen and reheated them in a special oven. Any restaurant owner would have been pleased with the size and equipment of the kitchen. The kitchen alone seemed to be as big as a 2½ room prefabricated apartment and all the walls were tiled in white right up to the top.

Michael tried to make me acceptable to his parents by telling them that I was studying biology and chemistry. My parents immediately started asking me questions about what I thought about genetic engineering and how genetic manipulation could affect heredity. They must have thought I was stupid, because I couldn't give any scientifically sound answers. I felt intimidated and was unable to lighten the conversation. When we said goodbye later, the father thanked me for the beautiful picture I had painted. It left me speechless. Michael had simply given it away. I had painted it for me and my son. He couldn't just take it away from me. I wasn't able to clear up the mistake on the spot. But I would confront Michael and reclaim the painting.

January 21, 1971: Death of my mother

When I left my parents' house on Monday morning to go to the train, everything was still in perfect order. I'd had breakfast with my parents and my son and we'd hugged and said goodbye to each other. It was the same as always. My mother would soon be taking the little one to work at the kindergarten and I would be home again on Friday evening.

My mother had said to me in private: "We should celebrate your father's 55th birthday at the weekend. He's in a very bad way. Maybe it's his last birthday."

I understood the seriousness of the matter, because my father was really very ill. He was having more and more epileptic seizures, which were probably caused by the shrapnel from the war and eventually led to cancer. On the other hand, I was also looking forward to the family celebration at the weekend. Mother could bake wonderful cakes and it was nice to have all the relatives together again.

I didn't know that my mother had also become very ill in my absence. She had caught such a bad cold at work in the kindergarten that she had to lie in bed. My mother's sisters had looked after her sick parents and my little son as best they could.

But when I came home on Friday evening, I found a chaotic situation. My mother was lying apathetically in bed and was barely responsive. There was a sweet smell of urine. No one had realized that her life was in danger. All I could do was arrange for her to be admitted to hospital. But it was too late. My mother died of kidney failure in hospital on January 21, 1971, one day before my father's birthday, which we wanted to celebrate properly. She was only 49 years old.

My life also had to change drastically when my mother died. My mother had always taken a lot off my shoulders. Now I had to take responsibility for everything myself.

On the day of the funeral, I saw my brother and sister-in-law for the first time in 10 years. When they left in 1961, I was 14 years old. Now I was a grown woman. Little Uwe, whom I had taken out as a baby, was now 13 and there was another nephew, aged 7, who was born in the West.

I will never forget how my brother and I stood in front of our mother's open coffin.

"We will always stick together," we promised her.

1971/72: Direct studies under difficult conditions

I still had two years of study ahead of me. Now it seemed impossible for a student mother to finish her studies with a five-year-old son and a sick father. But life had to go on. My mother's younger sisters continued to offer me their help when I needed it. They were probably thanking their deceased older sister, who had raised them instead of their mother during their childhood and youth.

I lived in an apartment with my father and son. Early in the morning, I usually took my son to nursery school, went to the station and took the train for an hour and a half to Halle, where I was studying. During the journey there and back, I read my notes and studied for exams. In the afternoon, I picked Frank up from kindergarten and was a housewife and mother, cooking, cleaning, washing and taking care of everything that needed doing. I was determined to finish my studies. I needed the degree, if only for financial reasons. The aunts looked after my father when I wasn't there or picked the boy up from nursery. Working and earning money in the evenings after my studies and doing paperwork for Michael was no longer possible. I was also still shocked about the visit to his parents and that he had given my picture away. I broke up with him.

to talk to me againe came to me by car one evening to talk to me again. In the meantime, his time in the army was over and he was working at Mitteldeutscher Verlag. He stayed the night and drove back the next morning. He never came back. I didn't chase after him and left it at that.

1972: Sandra's birth and employment in a school

In April 1972, Sandra was born, shortly before I graduated.

In June, I was able to attend the diploma defense. I passed this last exam and was awarded a final certificate with the title of Diploma Teacher for Biology and Chemistry. I was happy that I had mustered up the strength to successfully complete my studies.

I started teaching in September 1972 and the problems continued. Michael denied paternity and did not acknowledge his daughter. In the meantime, he was living with another woman. It took another 2 years of court hearings before his paternity was officially confirmed. The court hearings always took place at the defendant's place of residence, so I had to travel there by train for hours with the baby. One of my aunts usually went with me and looked after the baby when I was in the courtroom. I also had to sue to get my oil painting back. With a baby, a schoolchild and a sick father, it was very difficult to prepare thoroughly for lessons. To make matters worse, I had to cycle to the school in the neighboring village. But I only had one chance: keep going and don't despair.

Early in the morning, I took the bike in one hand and the baby carriage in the other and pushed both to the crèche, where I dropped the little one off until the afternoon. Frank went to school on his own, which was almost opposite the apartment. Then I cycled the 8 km to school in all weathers. At the beginning I still had a mentor. After a year and a half, I had to pass the state examination (teaching exam).

To cope with the huge responsibility, I often had to go beyond my strength. To the outside world, I appeared strong and didn't let on. My aunts supported me, but they couldn't relieve me of the demands of my job. When I reached a mental low, I would often write letters late at night to my pen friend of many years in Nigeria, who was now married and had two children. Like everyone, he had his problems. Not only did he have to provide for his own family, he also had to support two of his brothers who had gone blind due to an illness. We probably kept writing to each other because we were able to express our worries and found it liberating. You didn't have to burden those around you with it and you felt much better because there was someone far away who would listen and respond with understanding.

I was 26 years old and would probably have to stay alone. I wasn't granted great love and an intact family.

1975: Failed teaching exam, children's health resort

I usually didn't have enough time for everything I needed to do. Some things I could only do superficially. One day before the chemistry teaching exam, my father was in a very bad way. He had epileptic seizures again and severe pain in his back. I had to call the family doctor, who then had him taken to hospital.

When the practical chemistry exam took place at school the next morning, I was very nervous. I hadn't had time to try out the experiment I wanted to present the day before.

An exam board of three people sat at the back of the classroom and took notes. I had planned to carry out an experiment with sodium and water and prove that the result of the reaction was caustic soda and hydrogen.

I first added a universal indicator to a glass basin of water, which turned the water green. Then I let some sodium flit back and forth on the surface of a glass basin. You could see that the water turned blue. This meant that an alkali had formed. The experiment did not go any further. Suddenly there was a huge bang with a spark and the glass of water shattered. I ran out of the classroom in a panic because I knew straight away that I had failed my teaching exam.

With immediate effect, I was no longer allowed to work as a biology and chemistry teacher. Worse than the failed experiment was the accusation that I had left the pupils alone in a dangerous situation. Although no one was hurt, I had to realize that the examination board was right.

I then worked in shifts at a children's health resort, partly as an educator and partly as a teacher in various grades, so that the children at the resort could keep up with the school curriculum. The work was varied. I was able to sing with the children, do arts and crafts, play sports or tell historical stories during city tours.

I was now 30 years old, had a son of 11 and a daughter of 5. I loved my children more than anything and was glad that they existed. They gave me the strength to cope with my stressful life. Sometimes it seemed to me that I wasn't raising the children, they were raising me. As their mother, I had to grow up quickly. I was sent from the children's spa home to a 14-day puppetry course in Leipzig. I later made stick puppets or crumple puppets with the children at the spa and performed impromptu plays whose stories the children invented themselves. The dialog depended on how the puppets were designed, e.g. whether they looked ridiculous, stupid, arrogant or proud.

I didn't have an easy time with my father at home. After my mother died, he took to the bottle more and more often and I wasn't strong enough to stand up to him or even help him. I was very unhappy about it. I was also burdened by the thought that my studies, which I had gone through with many hardships, had become pointless.

1976: Critics of the regime

I was invited to a work colleague's birthday party, where a lot of young people gathered. There was not only a party, but also a lot of discussion.

I got to know Wolfgang that evening. Through him, I learned a lot of things that were not publicly known. He was fascinated by Wolf Biermann and said: "Biermann says in his songs what many people think. He gets to the heart of the zeit-geist." He had recently witnessed Biermann's performance in the Nikolai Church in Prenzlau, which the Stasi had not heard about in advance. He was supposedly friends with Wolf. If I wanted, he'd like to take me with him once, in private. Perhaps the beginning of December would suit? At the moment, Biermann was in Cologne for a concert.

After the Cologne concert, however, Wolf Biermann was no longer allowed to enter the country because of his songs critical of the GDR. He was expatriated. As a result, there was no more meeting with him and the story with Wolfgang soon came to an end. But from then on, I followed the news more closely. It didn't take much and I would have been introduced to the dissident circles myself.

Twelve well-known writers and artists from the GDR (Stefan Hermlin, Christa Wolf, Gerhard Wolf, Heiner Müller, Volker Braun, Erich Arendt, Jurek Becker, Sarah Kirsch, Rolf Schneider, Stefan Heym and Günter Kunert) protested against Biermann's expulsion. They had written a letter to Erich Honecker and wanted to have it printed in the party newspaper *Neues Deutschland*. When this was not approved, they had the letter published in West Germany. In this way, the people of the GDR found out through television what they were not supposed to know.

Robert Havemann, a former comrade-in-arms of Honecker and former professor of physical chemistry at Humboldt University in Berlin, also wrote a letter to the Chairman of the State Council about the expatriation and had the text published in the West German magazine *Der Spiegel at* the same time. Havemann had been stripped of his teaching position and placed under house arrest since the 1960s.

Other critics of the regime soon emerged. The population took notice. Popular actors such as Manfred Krug and Armin Müller-Stahl left the GDR. Many critics of the regime also came from the ranks of the Protestant church, such as Pastor Rainer Eppelmann, who organized blues masses in Berlin Friedrichshain and thus attracted many young people. Shortly before his death, Havemann called for disarmament in East and West together with Pastor Eppelmann in the Berlin Appeal. Something had to happen. It was in the air. You could literally breathe it in. People no longer wanted to be locked up and patronized.

1977: Relocation and a new start
I had heard from a work colleague that teachers for science subjects were being sought around Berlin. I phoned the local district school inspector and told him about the failed exam. He said: "If you have completed your studies, then you can also teach." I took the risk of moving with the children and tried to make a fresh start. The aunts continued to look after my sick father as best they could.

I started working as a teacher again in 1977. I taught biology and chemistry and often substituted for other subjects, such as art education and English. I was happy in my job, but I couldn't find happiness and love with a partner.

July 14, 1979: Death of my father
From a distance, my relationship with my father had improved somewhat. Unfortunately, he died of cancer during the school vacations in 1979, when I was visiting him with the children. I blamed myself for not being with him during the most difficult time of his life.

My parents had done everything for me and supported me as long as they could. I had had the best parents I could ever have. Now I could only be sad about the loss and look back with gratitude.

I had to take care of the funeral, inform my brother in the West and do everything that had to do with the death. I had once read somewhere: Writing is help against death. I had already discovered that myself. I had to stay active and positive. So I kept writing so as not to despair. In sad times, I often even distracted myself by coming up with funny verses or short stories.

I was sure that I could have written entire novels. But I didn't have the time or money, and I probably didn't have the appropriate literary training.

I couldn't let go of the idea. After all, if I had been writing letters, poems and stories all my life, why not books? Of course, I and the children wouldn't have been able to make a living from writing. I would still have to work in my profession. But maybe it was worth a try. I joined a circle called "Writing Workers" and occasionally read some of my poems and stories, always the harmless and unassailable ones. We criticized and and improved our little works and the leader of the circle, children's book author Klaus Mehler, published an anthology that included one of my poems. But I continued to write hundreds of other poems and stories for the drawer.

Remote learning at the Literature Institute
I applied to the "Johannes R. Becher" Literature Institute in Leipzig, which was run by Max Walter Schulz, for a three-year correspondence course specializing in poetry/prose and was accepted. I submitted a story entitled *Kirschplantage*[23] as my final thesis. It was a break-up story that I had written very lovelessly, because I had to stay true to the line and it wasn't easy to suppress my true feelings. Nevertheless, I completed the three-year correspondence course with a diploma. But I gave up the idea of ever publishing a book. Writing like Christa Wolf, whose novel *The Divided Sky* was on everyone's lips and highly praised, was not possible for me. I couldn't contribute to improving our society if I had to present a dubious ideology as the only true one. If I wanted to write something for the public, I had to be able to express

---

23 Cherry Orchard

my own view of the world. This required courage and honesty, but freedom of opinion was not a basic right in the GDR.

At home, the children and I discussed the grievances in the country and we had many ideas for improving the economic and political situation. But we didn't have the courage, or rather we couldn't afford to express our thoughts publicly, because criticism meant that you were hostile to the state and had to accept disadvantages.

However, my adolescent son dared to write in a civics test: "Karl Marx would turn over in his grave" or "How can I compare West Germany and the GDR if I'm never allowed to go to West Germany?" The principal of his school arranged a discussion between me, my son and someone from State Security immediately after school. Frank and I didn't have a chance to talk beforehand. Fortunately, the discussion went smoothly and there were no further consequences for the time being. It could have happened that I lost my job and our livelihood was no longer secure.

Frank had naturally attracted attention. In the last school year, he was transferred to a school in the neighboring town. He had to cycle there every day. In 1982, he finished the 10th grade there with good results.

The children had to realize that it was better to hold back their own opinions so as not to get into trouble. You couldn't win in an authoritarian state. The party was always right.

1983: Udo Lindenberg's "special train" to Pankow

When Udo Lindenberg sang his song *Sonderzug nach Pankow* in 1983, the people smiled. He seemed to be the only West German singer who sang for the East German people. He called Honecker an Oberindianer, who secretly puts on his leather jacket in the toilet and listens to West German radio, but won't let him perform in the Palace of the Republic.

In October 1983, Lindenberg was allowed to sing in the Palast der Republik after all, like all the other "Schlager monkeys". However, he was only allowed to perform in front of a select audience. His fans were held back by the police outside the palace.

The GDR government did not trust Lindenberg. He was closely monitored during his stay.

In 1987, Lindenberg gave Honecker a leather jacket on his first visit to the FRG, in Wuppertal.

My teaching staff were indignant. How could a pop singer put himself on the same level as a head of state and even be on first-name terms with him? An impossibility! In any case, Udo Lindenberg had triggered a discussion among the population. People made fun of those in power. His song became an anthem against the building of the Wall and the narrow-mindedness of the state.

1988: Invitation from the University of Sokoto/Nigeria

Ibrahim had sent me an official invitation from the University of Sokoto, an original that was stamped and signed. It stated that I had been invited for a friendly visit based on 25 years of correspondence and that they would pay for my accommodation and food.

I had been waiting tables at closed events as a part-time job and had painstakingly saved up the money for the flight.

I wrote a letter to the Minister for National Education, Margot Honecker, in the hope of a positive decision.

The answer came back quickly. The trip was rejected. Foreign currency had to be spent on business trips. There was no reason to travel to Nigeria. I didn't want to accept this and looked for another way to get the trip through after all.

June 1989: Honecker consultation

At the beginning of June, I had traveled to Berlin after making a telephone appointment. I now tried to get a permit for the trip to Nigeria at the Honecker office. I would then fly from Berlin Schönefeld to Sofia on July 22, 1989 at 7:15 p.m. and land in Lagos at 5:20 a.m. I had written to Ibrahim and hoped to have a legal basis in the Helsinki Final Act of 1975. In the meantime, business trips to capitalist countries abroad could be approved.

I had expected that many people would come to the Honecker consultation with their concerns and that there would certainly be a long queue. But the opposite was the case. After I rang the bell, someone opened the door and let me in. A middle-aged state secretary stood at a sufficient distance behind a kind of reception desk and asked me to take a seat in the waiting room. Then he went out and left me alone in the whitewashed room with the picture of the Chairman of the State Council. I had the unpleasant feeling that he was watching me. After an hour and a half, the State Secretary came back and announced from behind his barrier: "As long as political conditions require it, no foreign trips to capitalist countries will be authorized. There is no legal basis for this."

It sounded like a mockery, but I still tried to talk to him person to person. "Listen, I got an invitation from a university. I teach English as a dead language, like Latin, because I've never been to an English-speaking country. A colleague of mine teaches French. She got permission to travel to Paris! Why not me?" He looked down at me uncomprehendingly and just shrugged his shoulders: "I can't say anything else."

He made an unmistakable polite gesture and I stood outside the door again.

I had long believed that there had to be common sense even

among civil servants. But as everything went its socialist way, the happiness of an individual counted for nothing. individual counted for nothing. I felt something developing inside me that I had never known before: hatred. I had been humiliated and kicked out the door like a little dog. But I had held on. You just shouldn't underestimate me. From now on, I would fight against the state laws that forbade friendships and travel to foreign people.

Budapest: Juli 1989

The trip to Nigeria had come to nothing. My children, now 23 and 17 years old, had their own ideas about vacations. When they were little, we had often gone on vacation together. Once we had even met up with my brother's family in Hungary, in Fonyód, and spent a few days together.

I was depressed. Everything around me was gray in gray, the houses, the streets, the exhaust fumes, the dust in the air. I just wanted to get away and think better thoughts.

If not a trip to Nigeria, then back to Hungary. Hungary meant sun, color, relaxation.

However, Julia was spending her summer vacation with her family in Italy that year. My colleague Ilse from work had suggested: "If you want, you can spend a few days with us from July 20. We're staying at the international campsite in Budapest. We can bring a small one-man tent for you.

Without giving it much thought, I accepted the offer and took the night train from Berlin on July 20, 1989, arriving at Keleti station in Budapest shortly after 9. As soon as I arrived, I went to the international campsite, which was centrally located and beautifully surrounded by greenery. But Ilse's name wasn't on the registration form. Maybe something had gone wrong. Then I had to ask again later.

As I walked through Budapest, I noticed that there were a lot of young people with backpacks in the city and a lot of Trabants with GDR license plates parked in the streets, some even without license plates. I remembered Budapest very differently. Of course, I had been following the news and knew that many vacationers wanted to take their chance to get to the West since the Hungarians had dismantled the border fences with Austria.

The weather was pleasant, a little cloudy, but the sun was shining. I walked across the busy Margaret Bridge and from there to Margaret Island. I had to get the day over somehow. I had been to the beautiful thermal baths, the Japanese garden and the water tower with Julia years before. I bought a piece of langosch and a bottle of water at a stall along the way. A group of young people were camped out under the trees in the park, surrounded by luggage. They were chatting, laughing and passing a bottle around. I looked for a shady spot on the grass, put my head on my rucksack and fell asleep.

After recovering for a few hours, I decided to go back to the station and put my rucksack in a locker for the time being.

The station was packed with people. Many were stretched out on the floor like homeless people, sleeping or resting. There was no free locker to be found. As I walked past a disappointed group of young people squatting on the floor, I was approached by someone: "Would you like to join us? Then we could get you a locker."

"What do you mean?" I replied incredulously.

"Well, you look like you don't want to go back to the GDR either, do you?" I stood still for a while and listened to what the young people had to say. Lockers were too expensive in the long run. To avoid having to pay again every 24 hours,

69

they manipulated the locks by turning back the timer with a hairpin and then placing several pieces of luggage in one locker. This allowed them to keep the locker for as long as they wanted and save some money, which they didn't have enough of anyway. At night they slept on the train, which was ready for the journey to Berlin at 2 a.m., but didn't leave until around 6 a.m.. Shortly before departure, they got off the train again. It was not yet clear how they would manage to get to Austria or West Germany. But they wanted to find out. I looked into the tired but expectant faces of the people getting off.

Then I wished them good luck and said: "I'm not planning to leave the GDR, I have two children at home."

I walked back towards the city center with my heavy backpack and asked again at the international campsite. But Ilse hadn't been registered yet. I thought about what I could do.

I had been allowed to exchange 400 marks, of which 12 days were in forints and 2 days in Czech crowns. I couldn't afford a hotel room with that. I would have lost 100 marks in one night. I had to remember that I also had to buy something to eat and drink.

The year before, I had spent the night with Gesine, a former colleague, in Budapest in Julia's brother's bachelor apartment. But it was now taken. We had met "Wototok", a man from Budapest who had turned out to be a good city guide. He really wanted to learn German because his brother worked in the GDR, in Eisenhüttenstadt, and he also intended to go there. His real name was Joszsef Nagy, but as he kept asking: "Voltatok itt? (Have you been here before?), he had given himself the name. I still had his address in my wallet.

Now Wototok could perhaps be the savior in need.

I went to Deák Ferenc Tér and asked which bus went to

Kerulet. I got off at Hadrianus utca, which was in a pre-fabricated housing estate. The address given was easy to find. I rang Nagy's doorbell. An older man opened the door. It was his father. I showed him the address in his son's handwriting. He didn't understand German, but he knew that I was friends with his son. He invited me in and seemed inconsolable. Jozsef was currently in the GDR with his brother. I didn't dare ask if I could stay with him for a few days. He would certainly have agreed, because he was a polite man and had even offered me a "kis fekete kave"[24]. I soon said goodbye and drove back. I asked again at the campsite. But Ilse hadn't turned up.

What should I do now? I considered my options. Maybe Ilse had had to cancel the trip or could only leave later. After all, there was no chance of contacting me.

The teenage locker crackers had at least offered me an option. I would wait a few more days and ask at the campsite. Maybe Julia would be back from Italy by then and I could go to Zalaegerszeg.

During the day I could go to Margaret Island, lie in the sun or wander through the city, eat ice cream or langosch and melon and go to the Fisherman's Bastion, where admission was free. I could look at the parliament from there or watch the tourist buses that drove into the Danube and became swimming buses. When it got cold and dark, I had to go back to the station and spend the night in the train like the others. I just had to get off in time.

But it didn't turn out to be that easy. The weather changed the very next day and it started to rain all day. I took refuge in the large department store near Nuygati station and rode

---

24 small black coffee

71

up and down the escalators, looking at clothes and sweaters that I couldn't afford, watching well-dressed women who spoke Austrian and tried on shoes that they could afford.

In der Nacht stieg ich in den bereitgestellten Zug nach Berlin. But there was no question of sleeping. The hard two-seater seats were far too short to stretch out for any length of time. All you could really do was sit there and close your eyes. I had spent two nights like that and was completely exhausted and frozen through.

When it was still raining on the third day and I got chills and a fever, I gave up. It had just been stupid of me to go to Hungary and rely on others.

I just wanted to go home and sleep in. On the third night, I just stayed on the train, which left for Berlin at around 6.00 am.

12.08.1989: Vacation and alone at home

I had recovered from my cold in Hungary and could still have stayed in bed. But the light-colored curtains let the sunlight through and I woke up.

Mikosch, our tabby cat, had been sleeping at my feet. He had crept in unnoticed. He usually slept with Pussi, his mother, in the garage.

"Come on, you crazy cat!" I said and took him in my arms. I cuddled him a little, taking him in my arms and letting my long blond hair fall over his head. It was as if he understood very well that I needed comforting. He gently touched my face with his velvet paws and purred contentedly.

"You're an incredibly great cat. How lucky we are to have you!" I put him down and he followed me into the kitchen.

As I put his favorite food in his bowl, chopped beef rumen, Pussi miaowed loudly outside in the yard. I let her in through the kitchen door, which was also the front door. The two cats ate together from a bowl, or rather, they pulled the pieces of rumen out of the bowl and then wolfed them down from the floor.

I looked at the kitchen clock. It was only seven o'clock.

"Never mind," I thought, "I can still finish writing the letter to Ibrahim before the postbox is emptied."

I tied my hair up with a scrunchie and went into the shower. The children's dirty towels, which had been gone for a week, were still hanging in the bathroom. I opened the washing machine door, threw them in with the pile of bed linen and turned on the washing machine.

I envied my older children, Frank and Sandra, who had left for their summer vacation, happy and free, like migratory birds. Frank and a few friends had gone camping on the Baltic Sea on their souped-up mopeds and Sandra had taken the train to Wilfried in Mecklenburg. Wilfried was her first boyfriend.

I finished the letter to Ibrahim, stuck a stamp on the airmail letter and took it to the letterbox just around the corner. I was lucky. The Postbus for the 8 o'clock delivery was just pulling up. I bought two fresh hot rolls from the bakery next door, brewed myself a cup of black Turkish coffee and ate the two rolls with butter and strawberry jam.

From time to time I looked out of the window at the courtyard of the house. A large patch of sunlight slowly crept over the gate and filled the courtyard more and more.

I wondered whether I should perhaps put a lounger there to sunbathe and read a book. But I quickly gave up the idea as the landlord drove his Wartburg out of the garage to wash it in the yard.

To avoid the temptation to sink into endless brooding, I decided to go for a short bike ride on my folding bike.

I rode down the tarred road to the forest. On the right-hand side, behind a double barbed wire fence, was the Soviet airfield.

Sometimes a large transport plane landed there, an Ilyushin or an Antonov. But there wasn't much going on there today. Some soldiers were working on a smaller plane, probably a MiG 25, some distance away on the landing field. I wasn't very interested in fighter planes like that. But if you lived here, you heard something about it at some point. You just took it in. I was able to take a look inside the nearest open hangar, which looked like a green overgrown hill from the outside. The plane inside seemed to be the same as the one on the runway.

"Karasho, tovarishch,"[25] I heard as I drove past.

I had to laugh to myself.

"Ras, dwa, tri, towarischtsch kompanie! ", Frank had once ordered behind his hand as the Soviet soldiers marched through the town in step. As far as I know, there was no contact between the townspeople and the Soviet soldiers. It was probably not desired by the government either. An attempt to accommodate Soviet and German families in a joint new housing development failed. Many people did not like the Soviet occupiers. There was the organization Deutsch Sowjetische Freundschaft, which I had also joined. You only paid a monthly or annual membership fee.

As a little girl, Sandra had once thrown raw eggs onto an aeroplane and then proudly announced: "Do you know that you can fry eggs on airplanes standing in the sun?"

Much of what the children had done behind my back they only told me years later, some perhaps never.

I pedaled steadily. My folding bike wasn't exactly suitable as

---

25 Good, comrade

a racing or trekking bike. I usually only rode it to school, and then my thoughts turned to the subject matter I had to teach. Today, however, pedaling the bike always made me think about myself. I felt like I was living in a labyrinth. I wanted to get out of it. But was there even a way out?

I cycled the long tarred road to the next village through the pine forest without paying attention to my surroundings. I hadn't really noticed the barracks surrounded by barbed wire or the Soviet housing estate in the middle of the forest, I had passed the forest lake, deer in the woods, a lot of red toadstools, old ivy-covered trees. Nothing could distract me from my sad thoughts.

Around midday I was back home, parked the bike in the yard, went into the house and started to pass the time with the banjo. Strangely enough, I kept coming up with folk songs that I could easily rewrite to vent my anger. *"Auf der Mauer, auf der Lauer sitzt ne kleine Wanze"*[26], that had such a nice double meaning! Or: *"Hänschen klein, ging allein in die fremde Botschaft rein"*[27], *"Kommt ein Vogel geflogen"*[28], whereby I thought of the lawyer who arranged the ransom of those wishing to leave the country with the FRG, "No more beautiful country at this time than ours far and wide. Where we find each other under the lime trees..." In my mind I was on Unter den Linden in Berlin. I wrote the lyrics in a little booklet and wondered whether I hadn't tried everything for the trip to Nigeria after all. Maybe I just hadn't found the right address yet. After all, some people had already managed to get permission to travel abroad. Were they all Stasi employees? The physics teacher at my school had even spent a few weeks in

26 A little bug sits on the wall, on the lookout
27 Little Hans went into the foreign embassy alone
28 When a bird flies

West Germany the year before, even though he was far from being a pensioner. When the new school year started, he hadn't come back. It was rumored that he had been exposed as a spy in the West. Now they had to negotiate so that he could come back. Why some were allowed to travel and others not was quite mysterious. Of course, I didn't want to be a Stasi employee or a spy, but perhaps I should try again with the Minister of the Interior. Maybe he would approve the trip to Nigeria.

So I sat down at my desk and wrote a letter to the Minister of the Interior.

Letter to the Minister of the Interior

Dear Minister,

I am requesting permission to travel to Nigeria. The reason is an invitation from the University of Sokoto (see attachment)

I have been in correspondence with the Secretary of the University, who works for the UN, among others, for almost 25 years.

I have been working in the teaching profession for 17 years and also teach English. For me, a stay in an English-speaking country would be comparable to a further education course.

In accordance with the regulation on travel abroad by citizens of the GDR dated 30.11.88, my trip could be considered a study trip.

As some of my fellow teachers had already received permission to travel abroad, this should also apply to me.

However, after discussions with the VP office in my place of residence and with officials from your ministry, it seems to be much easier to obtain permission to leave the country permanently than to visit a foreign country.

I would like to make it clear that I do not wish to apply to leave the GDR, but to travel abroad to Nigeria.

Yours sincerely

Please find enclosed the necessary documents

3 passport photos

Invitation from the host (University of Sokoto)

3 x travel documents

Sunday, August 13, 1989: 28th anniversary of the Berlin Wall

The wall clock ticked loudly into the silence. I wondered if it would always be like this from now until the end of my days? The children flew out of the nest, started their own lives, had friends, dreams and plans for the future. But I, at forty-two, was leading a lonely and unhappy life, with the occasional sex adventure, but nothing lasting.

I wanted to finally meet Ibrahim in person, the person who had given me support in life after my brother had gone to the West and my parents had died prematurely. I only had this one person in whom I could confide everything since my childhood, for almost 25 years. The people around me were colleagues, neighbors, acquaintances, parents and students, people who knew nothing about my soul and my dreams. To the others, I was a teacher and a mother, nobody knew the real me. I myself only suspected that there was something inside me that was me. But it had never been able to develop. I had never existed as a person. Only now, when the children went their own ways, did I finally want to rediscover my life, which had been lost somewhere between childhood and adulthood.

I felt terribly lonely. My soul was screaming. Nobody asked whether I was happy with my life or not. I would have liked to have an intact family. But I couldn't find a father for two children anyway.

The children had been the most important thing for me in the last twenty years. Was the time now coming when they would not only go their own ways, but soon leave home for good?" Sandra was doing an apprenticeship as a waitress. But she hadn't chosen this apprenticeship. It had been forced upon her. She was actually very talented artistically and had already published a drawing in the town's local calendar at the age of ten. In the meantime, she was earning extra money by painting T-shirts for friends and acquaintances, with portraits that she usually copied from passport photos. The similarities were unmistakable. She was very good at it.

In the 9th grade, I went with her to a master teacher for lettering and was accepted by him for training. But then he decided on someone else.

I objected to the careers planning office that Sandra should learn a profession that didn't suit her. I was told: "If the director of the school would confirm that your child really is as artistically gifted as you say, perhaps something can be done." But the principal didn't stand up for Sandra. He was the same principal who had arranged for Frank to change schools. His opinion was: "Sandra should first learn to subordinate herself and a career as a waiter is just the right thing for that."

Sandra was very disappointed at first. But then she made a virtue out of necessity. Due to her exceptional performance, she was allowed to complete her vocational qualification six months earlier. She used the time she had gained by taking an English course (year 11) at the adult education center.

She vowed not to work a single day as a waitress and continued to paint T-shirts based on motifs provided by her clients. But of course she wanted to find a second educational path and study design in Berlin at some point. Sandra was an extremely strong-willed girl and it was to be expected that she would go her own way. Her boyfriend, who was five years older, encouraged her in her plans. At some point, they would both go to Berlin to study. They had aspirations and goals and seemed like they would make a good couple. But of course no one could see into the future.

Frank did well with his training as a bricklayer. He was the best of his group. He once said: "The principal couldn't ruin my life. I only ever wanted to be a bricklayer. I can see what I've achieved every day, I can show someone the house or garage I've built. I couldn't imagine being a baker, doing the same thing every day and everything always being eaten away? No thanks."

Despite occasional setbacks, the children seemed to be following their future path. But what else was I doing with my life? I had been through enough failed relationships. But being alone wasn't an option either. It gave you the strangest ideas and could make you depressed.

I switched on Radio DDR II. The Puhdys were singing "*Alt wie ein Baum möchte ich werden*"[29]. It was a very touching song. I hummed along quietly and my eyes fell on the large green baobab plant on the windowsill. The plant resembled the huge tree on the postcard that was stuck on the corkboard next to the calendar. Somewhere in the savannah of Nigeria, between the Sahara and the tropical rainforest, this plant grew as a huge tree. Sometimes, when hollowed out, it even served as a small goat pen. For me, the baobab was now more than just a green houseplant. It came from untouched, eternal nature and had become a symbol of hope and longing. The baobab was also the "Little Prince's" plant, which worried him because it could overgrow his little asteroid and burst with its roots.

---

29 I want to grow as old as a tree

My children only called the plant the money tree. But that was no contradiction to its symbolic value. I had already planted a hundred offspring in small pots. They were scattered all over the apartment, on windowsills, bookshelves and on the desk, as if hope could be multiplied a hundredfold. The saleswoman in the flower store around the corner wanted to take the plants when they were 15 cm tall and sell them in the store. I was supposed to get one mark per plant.

I had to smile for a moment. I could watch the cat through the window. He was sitting on the saddle of my bike as if he was about to ride off. I knocked on the window. As soon as the cat noticed, he jumped down and ran towards me through the kitchen door.

A butterfly had entered the kitchen and was fluttering around the room. It was an emperor butterfly. The cat jumped onto the chair to catch it.

"No, Mikosch! Leave the butterfly alone!" I pushed him aside. The butterfly had sat down on the baobab and closed its wings. I took it carefully between my thumb and forefinger and let it back out into the open.

It made me think of Mr. Winkler, who had probably planted a longing for Africa in my soul.

When the news came on, I switched off the radio. I no longer wanted to hear the Hungarian refugees being called traitors. I had experienced for myself what was happening in Budapest and could understand everyone who was running away.

I looked at my watch. It was just after 2.00 pm. The letter to the Minister of the Interior and the little booklet with the ten rewritten folk songs I had played on the banjo were still on the table. I hummed to myself: "There's a little bug sitting on the wall". Then I put the letter, booklet and banjo in my rucksack, put on a jacket and decided to go to Berlin.

Berlin Alexanderplatz

I got off at Alexanderplatz S-Bahn station and wanted to walk under the Linden trees to the Brandenburg Gate. The sun was burning like a furnace on the capital of the GDR. I had never been to Berlin on the anniversary of the Wall being built, but it seemed like a good date to be there. The sun was on the sphere of the television tower and dazzled me when I looked up. In fact, the reflection of a cross was clearly visible. "Ulbricht's memorial church", I thought, remembering the story that went around after the inauguration of the TV tower in 1969. Allegedly, Ulbricht was so angry about the cross that he had the architect interrogated by the Stasi. The idea was to find out whether the cross had been deliberately planned.

People were walking in all directions across the expansive Alexanderplatz, past the Fountain of Friendship between Nations and the World Time Clock. However, it seemed that not so many people were going into the Zentrum department store today, there was more movement towards the Rathauspassagen. A group of children sat on the steps to the restaurant and threw leftover bread rolls onto the pavement, whereupon a flock of pigeons and sparrows fluttered among the crowd. An observation camera high up on the House of State Security followed the goings-on in the square. It was burning hot. I joined the queue at the ice cream van and bought a soft ice cream. Suddenly I heard uproarious laughter and applause and thought I couldn't believe my eyes and ears. Two young men in FDJ shirts performed a ballet-like victory dance around the fountain. Full of enthusiasm, they waved a papier-mâché hammer and sickle above their heads. They pirouetted around their own axis, bent down, spreading the FDJ shirt from their bodies with one hand like a lace skirt, then looked heroically up to the sky and finally leapt elegantly into the water of the fountain, which splashed up high and soaked the bystanders. The applause died down when a police car suddenly appeared. The young men were arrested without resistance. The spectators remained silent. The car drove off and people went their separate ways as if nothing had happened. I had never seen a performance like that before. Unbelievable! People dared to make fun of the system in public.

A crowd of people queued for tickets at the television tower. Anyone who came to Berlin must have at least had a look at the sights from the viewing platform and at the roof of the West Berlin Springer publishing house, which could be seen directly below and was reminiscent of a swastika. Whether this was the architect's intention remains just as questionable. You could see all the way to the Brandenburg Gate from above and even make out the Reichstag building behind the wall. I walked through the Rathauspassagen, past the red town hall and the Palace of the Republic. On the other side of the street, the cathedral shone with its green dome and golden cross on top. I had seen it being restored for years and now felt a strange sense of pride that the work had been completed. I continued along the right-hand side of the street, leaving the Museum Island with the Bode and Pergamon museums behind me, and crossed the Spree at Marx-Engels-Platz. I almost didn't notice the river. The Spree was completely encased in concrete and looked more like a large sewer. I stopped for a moment and looked down at the dark water where a few mallards were swimming. As always, two soldiers stood at the New Guardhouse with their rifles over their shoulders in a stern posture, looking straight ahead. They guarded the eternal fire in memory of the victims of fascism and militarism. The equestrian statue of the Prussian King Frederick II, over ten meters high, stood in the middle of the street and divided the magnificent avenue "Unter den Linden" with its shady rows of green trees. The "Old Fritz" looked down calmly on the passers-by and cars that drove past him on the right towards the Brandenburg Gate and returned on the left.

Unter den Linden

I sat down on a bench under the lime trees. The air was shimmering with heat. Here in the shade, it was more or less bearable. For a while, I wondered whether I should stick to my plan to cause a stir. But I couldn't see any other way to push through my travel plans. I had been rebuffed too many times and I couldn't give up any more. The battle had long since begun and I wanted to win it.

I unpacked my banjo and began to quietly play seemingly innocuous folk songs: "Auf der Mauer auf der Lauer sitzt `ne kleine Wanze" and "Kein schöner Land in dieser Zeit". Pedestrians walked past and wondered. It was not customary to sit on a bench and play songs. There were no street musicians, beggars or peddlers in the GDR. But no police appeared. Instead, a group of young people approached curiously and listened. "Why are you actually doing this?" asked a woman of about thirty with a serious face. After I had explained my intention, she said: "I can understand you, but I would ask you not to throw your life away carelessly. I speak from my own experience. I spent three years in the Hohenfels women's prison. I'm telling you, you'll be psychologically destroyed if you have to go in there. I now suffer from insomnia and anxiety. I'm now fighting to get my little boy back. They put him in a home. I was sent to prison as a 'political' person, but I was treated worse than the mass murderer who killed Jewish children with her own hands. Please give up your plan. You can't win."

The people moved on. I hadn't dared to ask why the woman had been sent to prison, but I pocketed my banjo. I had never heard of Hohenfels women's prison and had never thought about people who had been politically imprisoned. But when I looked into the woman's eyes, I knew that she had spoken the truth.

To the Brandenburg Gate

Thoughtfully, I walked on towards the Brandenburg Gate, my rucksack with the banjo over my shoulder. I only glimpsed the buildings to my left and right: the State Library, the House of the Trade Union, the Hotel Unter den Linden, the House of the Central Council of the FDJ. I let myself drift along with the stream of passers-by. Most of them were young people, teenagers or couples holding hands. I felt connected to them. They were like-minded people who had gathered here in a kind of silent protest. They didn't know each other and didn't belong to any organized group. They probably just came to see if anything was happening on the 28th anniversary of the construction of the Wall, officially called the "anti-fascist protective wall".

People walked alone or in pairs and yet it seemed as if it would be easy to suddenly join together in a large demonstration. After all, there had already been several protest demonstrations and arrests on Alexanderplatz since the fraudulent local elections on the seventh of May. It was simply inconceivable that 99 percent of voters would have re-elected the SED. Many voters' names had not been put on the electoral lists in the first place because they had either applied to leave

84

the country or had not turned up to vote the year before. In retrospect, it was almost incomprehensible to me that the arrest of the two young dancers on Alexanderplatz had been accepted by the spectators without protest.

My attention was suddenly drawn to the building entrances to the right and left of the street. There was a man in uniform in almost every one. Most of them were young men, barely older than Frank, almost boyish still. Passers-by and police officers watched each other. The closer I got to the Brandenburg Gate, the denser the police presence became.

The air was charged. Something was brewing here, like an approaching thunderstorm. You could feel it with all your senses.

Anyone who dared to walk along here today could only have the intention of provoking. The police were prepared for this.

At the Brandenburger Gate

A rope had been stretched across the street about 30 meters in front of the Brandenburg Gate. A policeman asked people not to go any further. Most of the young people walking along here had only been born when the Wall was already up. They didn't know Berlin any differently. They were a little rebellious, but then turned around and walked back towards the city center. One young woman, however, could not be held back, laughed hysterically and climbed over the rope. The policeman remained calmly in place and did nothing about it. I stood behind the barrier for a while and watched the game. The woman walked across the open space with her head held high, as if she were on a stage. The Brandenburg Gate and the three-metre-high wall behind it looked like a huge prison backdrop to the opera Nabucco. Fenena, daughter of the Babylonian king Nabucco, and the captive Hebrews are to be led to the place of execution. The condemned sing the longing prisoners' chorus, softly at first, then swelling louder and louder. But the woman did not appear. The play played out differently, without the freedom chorus and the liberation of the Hebrews. As soon as three people stood together, they were asked to disperse.

Directly in front of the Brandenburg Gate, behind another barrier, two men knelt and lit candles. The border guards, who were standing directly behind the rope, watched and let them go. Two police cars were parked to the left and right of the square. They kept an eye on the situation. Meanwhile, on the green lawn between the Brandenburg Gate and the Wall, a lot of wild rabbits hopped around without a care in the world, going about the business of preserving their species and not allowing themselves to be disturbed at all. They had been living here for more than a hundred generations of rabbits and had learned that nothing would be done to them. The young woman who had been walking across the square was told to get into the emergency vehicle with other people. They were taken away. So that's what I had to do if I wanted to have my say and get rid of the letter to the Minister of the Interior.

Now I stepped into the spotlight. I ignored the words of the uniformed man next to me and walked across the open space, straight towards the men kneeling in front of the candles. I stopped next to a man on my right and asked why he was kneeling in front of the candle. He looked up at me and replied in a strangely familiar tone that surprised me: "I've been coming here every year since my friend was shot at the wall." The uniformed man behind the rope listened to the conversation. The man continued: "You don't seem to know me, but I often see you when you ride your bike to school. My niece told me that she has lessons with you." It turned out that he worked as a tractor driver on the LPG, not far from my school. I knew Steffi, his niece. I had never noticed him before. We smiled at each other. "Well then, see you next time." He went back to his devotions and I walked on. I would see him again one day and perhaps have a longer chat with him.

I noticed that there were other people who had lit candles and slowly walked over to the opposite side of the street, where the USSR embassy building was and a police car was parked. I noticed that they were keeping an eye on me, almost expecting me. I had wanted it that way. For two years I had been turned away everywhere by officials or secretaries. Now I wanted to take the final hurdle. I just couldn't give up until I had tried everything. I just wanted the police to finally arrest me. "Where there's a will, there's a way." "Fly, thoughts on golden wings." The Minister for Travel Affairs should decide in person. I wanted to know for sure. Did the decisions really come from the very top? I stood next to two young men who had also lit candles and started a conversation with them. I learned that many people from all parts of the country had come today to apply to leave the country. You were also one of them. One came from Gernrode in the Harz Mountains, the other from Magdeburg. Perhaps there was a chance of being expelled sooner if you were provocative. There had already been a big expulsion in January, either because they wanted to prevent unrest during the elections or because they needed foreign currency again. In any case, 200 unpopular con-temporaries had been sold to the West. One of them just said: "My grandfather lives in Essen. He is very ill and would like me to take over his carpentry business. I'm the only grandson who could do it." Then the emergency vehicle, a W 50, pulled up squealing next to us.

Together with the people who had lit candles, I was asked to hand over my ID and get into the car. Entertainment was forbidden.

Arrest and removal
The car drove off at high speed and turned right into a side street not far from the Brandenburg Gate. The journey only took a few minutes. The tractor driver sat next to me in the back seat. He looked extremely nervous. His hands were shaking. Suddenly he reached into his jacket pocket and pulled out a large knife, a kind of deer knife. I was startled, but didn't think he was going to hurt me. I made him understand with facial expressions and gestures that he should leave the knife in the car, possession of a weapon was punishable. After all, it was a weapon and as big as it was, you could kill someone with it.
He took my advice and left the knife in the car.
The car drove into a large courtyard surrounded by tall buildings with garages. There were a few other police cars in the square. We all had to get out of the car and were then taken one by one to an interrogation room on the ground floor.

Full body check and penalty seating with bright lights
A policewoman carried out a full body check on me for security purposes. I had to undress and be examined. Then I was allowed to get dressed again, but I had to hand over my rucksack with the banjo and the letter to the Home Secretary.
I was led to a higher floor, into a large corridor-like room. There were two long rows of chairs with backrests that abutted each other. An estimated forty people were already sitting there, illuminated by bright ceiling lights. At first it looked like a fun birthday party with a mixed audience. In a

moment, music would play and a musical chairs dance would begin, in which one chair would be taken away at a time, leaving one winner. But it wasn't going to be funny, nor would there be a winner.

Everyone had to sit quietly in their chairs and wait until they were led to the interrogation. It lasted many hours and went on all night. Anyone who had to go to the toilet had to report with their arm raised and was then escorted by a man in uniform. I couldn't see what the people who were picked up with me looked like. When you're sitting in a row and you're not allowed to move or turn around, it's not possible. A young woman was sitting next to me. I asked quietly under my breath, "Why are you here?" I learned that she and her husband had been arrested during a check. They didn't have their IDs with them. Unfortunately for them, they had left their baby with a neighbor and couldn't even notify her. The other person sitting next to them had applied to leave the country. Behind my back, two young men were whispering. They were the ballet dancers from Alexanderplatz. "I've seen you," I said, probably a little too loudly. The uniformed man at the entrance asked me to be quiet. Nevertheless, a smile went through the rows of chairs. Apparently I was only sur-rounded by criminals or criminals of this kind, who were all behaving in an extremely disciplined manner and practising silent protest.

The night became uncomfortably long on the hard chairs and in the bright light. I closed my eyes, nodded off and woke up again and again, startled.

At some point early in the morning, a man in uniform came into the room with a plate of greased slices and offered them to eat. One of the "delinquents" whispered: "Don't eat! They put something in there that gives you a stomach ache!"

It was a reddish spread that looked like a thinly scratched tea sausage. I had been arrested the night before at around 9 p.m. and was hungry. My stomach was growling loudly because I hadn't eaten since yesterday lunchtime.

I took a slice. The bread bent at the edges, was hard and dried out, as if it had been left over from a party the day before yesterday. It crunched when I bit into it. I could only conclude that it must be intentional to punish people. But it didn't give me a stomach ache.

14.08.1989: The interrogation

At around 8.00 a.m., I was taken for questioning by a young police officer. There were several uniformed officers in the relatively small, dark room who might have to intervene if necessary.

The room was dominated by an oversized brown desk with pens and documents on it, as well as a telephone and a tape recorder. In front of it was a simple chair. I was asked to take a seat. Behind the desk sat a middle-aged, high-ranking official with dark glasses and graying hair.

Without paying any attention to me, he began with the usual questions: name, place of birth, place of residence, occupation, etc. He was probably following a predetermined interrogation protocol, a sheet of paper in front of him. He must be a heavy smoker. His raspy, deep voice spoke for itself. It made me think of an ageing wolf.

Then came questions that were supposed to provide evidence. Only now did he look at me insistently, almost hostilely.

"Why did you apply to leave the country?"

"I didn't apply to leave the country."

The officer probably assumed that all the people who had been brought here had applied to leave the country and were therefore enemies of the state who had to be dealt with harshly.

"So, once again: why do you want to leave the country?"

I don't want to leave the country. I just want to apply for a trip abroad," I replied.

I tried to explain that I had a letter to the Minister of the Interior in my backpack as proof and would be happy if this letter was forwarded from here. The interrogator must have felt he was being made fun of and burst out laughing: "I'm not a postman. Why don't you do it yourself?"

"I would like to know why you have applied to leave the country?"

"I didn't," I repeated.

"Then why were you arrested at the anti-fascist barrier on August 13?"

"Because I wanted to hand in the letter for a trip abroad and didn't see any other chance."

"Why did you have to do this on August 13, when there was a chance of anti-state activities?"

"To be arrested, it had to be August 13th. Any other day would have been pointless."

I only had to answer questions and was not given the opportunity to explain myself. Compassion and understanding were not to be expected here. I felt contempt for this disrespectful, stupid treatment.

There was silence for a while. Then the officer shook his head, looked at me piercingly and said in an overly loud tone: "You can go home now. It should be clear to you that we will inform your district school board and that you will have to take the consequences."

Breakfast in a café in Berlin

Tired, angry and hungry, I left the police building with my rucksack at around 9.00 am. Some distance away, I spotted a pretty café on the other side of the street that looked like a small glass palace. I decided to go inside and have breakfast first. I felt a little dizzy. I floated across the street as light as an angel. I knew that feeling. Sometimes I suffered from low blood pressure. Then a cup of coffee could be helpful.

It was still early and the café was pretty empty. I had to be one of the first guests. I sat down at a table for four, right next to the large window overlooking the street and ordered a coffee and a sandwich with an egg.

Strangely enough, the café soon filled up and seats became scarce. A friendly, well-dressed, slightly older woman asked if she could sit with me. She ordered a piece of cake and a cup of coffee and we struck up a conversation.

I had never talked to strangers about my personal affairs before. But the woman made a trustworthy impression. She asked almost motherly: "Are you all right? You look kind of exhausted and pale."

Tears welled up in my eyes.

After that terrible night and the interrogation in the morning, it was good to talk to someone who would listen.

I told him what had happened to me yesterday at the Brandenburg Gate and that I wanted nothing more than to meet my writing friend in Nigeria in person, who was a secretary at the University of Sokoto. We had been writing to each other for 25 years. He was someone who was committed to human rights and international cooperation. I owed him a lot. Through our constant correspondence, I had learned English better and was even able to teach English at school and at the adult education center. But we would probably never see each other in our lives because the state forbade it. That was inhumane.

The woman had listened with interest and said: "Don't talk about inhumane. The state also does a lot of good things for its people. Just think of crèches, kindergartens, good schooling, university. Everyone can work according to their abilities. But every state also has its laws that you have to follow. If you don't, you're in big trouble. Don't get yourself into something you can't win. Get your travel thoughts out of your head if you don't want to be unhappy."

I couldn't accept that: "But it can't stay like that. If a friendship trip is something hostile to the state, then there's something wrong with the government!"

The woman shook her head: "I can only advise you to give up, otherwise you'll get into big trouble. Think about it!"

I finally thanked her for the conversation, paid, picked up my rucksack and went on my way along Unter den Linden towards the television tower.

I couldn't help but think about the woman. Something wasn't right. Maybe she was working with the Stasi, maybe she always went to this café to influence people who had just come in from interrogation. But why would the Stasi go to so much trouble?

I wasn't sure what to believe.

At Alexanderplatz I got on the S-Bahn to Bernau to take the train home from there.

Chance meeting

On the way from the station, I met Hanne, a young woman in her mid-thirties who was learning English in my adult education class. The age difference between us was hardly noticeable. I liked Hanne's outgoing, direct manner and if I hadn't been her teacher, we might have been friends.

In the first lesson, I asked all the participants why they wanted to learn English. The answers were almost all the same: English was an important language of communication. Hanne was the only one to say something different: "My husband and I have applied to leave the country. He's already been deported, I'm still sitting on packed suitcases. I want to make the most of the time. Studying distracts me."

"Nice to meet you," said Hanne. "I'm already looking forward to September, when the course continues." She looked at me a little thoughtfully: "Are you all right?"

I tried to smile: "I don't know what's going to happen at the moment."

"How is that? " Hanne asked in astonishment. "Don't you want to carry on?"

As there were a lot of people on the road and I could only briefly mention what had happened in Berlin, Hanne suggested that we should meet the next day. She quickly understood that there was a story that wasn't meant for all ears.

"Maybe I can help you."

15.08.1989: Allies

It was a very hot day. The thermometer on the wall of the house read 30 degrees in the shade. Hanne and I met at the ice cream parlor near the city park. As we shook hands, I said: "From now on, say 'du' please." Hanne laughed: "I'd love to." Not only did we like one other, we were now also allies. We bought ourselves an ice cream and sat down on a bench under a tree where we could talk without being disturbed.

Hanne understood that I could also lose my job. She told me that she had to give up her job as a physiotherapist after she applied to leave the country. But as she needed money and had contacts with showmen through her husband, she joined them. She took part in folk festivals around Berlin and sold waffles in a circus wagon. This was intended as a temporary income until she too was allowed to leave the country.

If I wanted to, I could come with her in the next few days and try out whether I could do such a job if I was banned from working. After all, I was still on vacation and my children were old enough to manage on their own.

I accepted the offer. Somehow I had to prepare myself for the uncertain future. Together with Hanne, this kind of trial period would not only be an adventure, but perhaps also the beginning of a friendship.

16.08-20.08.1989: Fairground Hoppegarten Hönow

We had traveled with Hannes Trabi[30], which made the journey easier. Then we didn't have to take the Berlin S-Bahn and U-Bahn network. However, the fairground was not far from the last subway station and if we wanted to, we could always take the train to the city center. But we were unlikely to find the time. We arrived at the accommodation in the early evening. It wasn't the circus caravan I was expecting, but a small rented room with two beds in a private house.

After we had stowed our things, we went to the fairground to see the new workplace.

Hanne was no stranger there. She was immediately greeted in a friendly manner by some of the showmen and reminded that a barbecue was planned for everyone the following evening.

Hanne confirmed that we would both be coming.

Everything was already set up on the fairground: bumper cars, chain carousel, air swing, Ferris wheel.

---

30 Trabant, a car produced in Zwickau.

There were raffle stalls of all kinds with dolls, teddy bears, cars and many other knick-knacks, shooting stands for firing plastic flowers and lots of stalls selling bratwurst, steak, potato pancakes, candy floss, glazed apples, roasted almonds, quark balls and ice cream. Hannes' waffle stand was right in the middle. It was a wagon made of light-colored wood, with a round roof and a hinged side panel that served as weather protection above and had a sales counter below. I was to operate the four waffle irons in the back from 10 a.m. tomorrow morning and Hanne would sprinkle them with powdered sugar and sell them. But we had to go to the wholesale market first thing in the morning to pick up the buckets of pancake batter we had ordered. "You don't need to worry, we'll manage," said Hanne.

A typical working day at the fair

At around 7 a.m. we drove along Landsberger Chaussee to the wholesale market, passing the Marzahn district on the left, whose large, sprawling apartment blocks stood out from the landscape like giant building blocks. The new buildings had only been built in the last twenty years around an old town center.

At the wholesale market, a friendly young salesman had already prepared the three buckets of dough and carried them to the Trabi. Hanne bought a few bottles of cream and a few packets of eggs and said: "We'll have to stir that in. Then it will taste much better."

At 10 o'clock sharp, the fairground filled up with crowds of people. Most of them were families with children who wanted to treat themselves and their offspring to something good before the vacation season was over. Loud music blared from the loudspeakers across the square. Each ride had its own music and volume, which mingled with the babble of voices of the people, the lottery ticket sellers and market criers. The sun was blazing down on the fairground. There was not a breath of wind. The temperature quickly climbed above 30 degrees. After Hanne had explained to me how to work the waffle irons, I filled one waffle iron after the other. I had to make sure that all the waffle irons were never ready at the same time, and it had to be done quickly because the queues at the counter were getting longer and longer. In addition to the high outside temperature, it was also a few degrees Celsius on the waffle irons. I was used to a lot of things and wasn't afraid of the work, but the unusually high temperature and the smell of the oil that I had to brush the irons with from time to time gave me a hard time. The heat was getting to my head and I felt a bit dizzy. The side door of the car was open, but it didn't let any air through. I had to keep taking a sip from the water bottle to stop myself falling over and keep up the pace. But Hanne wouldn't have been able to do it alone. She was glad that she had found me to help out. The stand was open from 10.00 am to 10.00 pm. Towards the evening, sales slowed down, but it was also necessary to slowly wind down. After all the showmen had finished their work, there was a communal barbecue before going to bed. Everyone had brought their own seating, stools, chairs or beer crates and formed a circle around the barbecue fire. The music had stopped everywhere and people ate, drank and talked to each other.

A bottle of Korn[31] was passed around. Normally I wouldn't drink alcohol, but Hanne had introduced me as her friend and was now looking at me shyly from the side: "Go on, it's

---

31 Schnapps

not poison, is it?" So I took a sip and shook myself: "Bah..."
Everyone looked at me and laughed. "It's all a matter of
habit," said one, another: "Once is always the first time."
The men in particular, who were in the majority, had found
their topic of conversation. "The women who are particularly
coy are the worst," they said. Then the name Beate Uhse
came up and someone they called Olli gave Hanne a small
gift: "Now that your husband isn't available and it was just
your birthday."
"Unpack! Unpack!" she was told. The unsuspecting Hanne
unwound several layers of paper, beaming with joy, until the
elongated blue object appeared."
Then she jumped up indignantly, slapped the bearer in the
face and said: "Maybe it's good for your wife if you can't get
it up!" She threw it at his feet.
The assembled company burst out laughing. I hadn't seen
what Hanne had been given and asked what it was.
Hanne shook her head. Olli now held up the blue thing, grinned
and pressed a button to set it in motion.
"My God, it's just a dildo from the Beate Uhse store."

Farewell to baking waffles

I was glad that I had survived the three days at the fairground. The intense heat, the sweet smell of oil and the hectic
12-hour work schedule took some getting used to. What I
had initially seen as an adventure and a possible escape
quickly turned out to be exhausting, exhausting work that
had shown me my limits.
"It's a shame, but I understand. Let's at least have a nice finish,"
said Hanne when I told her why. Hanne had reserved two
seats at Café Moskau. We took the S-Bahn to Karl-Marx-
Allee, which was still called Stalinallee in the 1960s.

The café was planned and furnished as a nationality restaurant. It was an important showpiece with many conference rooms that could be seen internationally. The entrance to the restaurant was at one corner of the building. A metal object from the first Sputnik was mounted on the roof above. Above and next to the entrance door was a large mosaic in blue, gray and brown depicting the lives of working people and families with children from the Soviet Union. There were various rooms in the building with names of other brother countries. In total, there were seats for more than 600 guests. The walls had wooden paneling and were decorated with Meissen porcelain. The establishment was probably not intended for the average person, but rather a central meeting place for people of distinction, for tourists from other countries, who could also meet GDR citizens here. I looked around and was amazed. People from all over the world seemed to be sitting at the tables and Hanne was no stranger here. The waitress who served us first exchanged a few private words with her. Hanne then ordered a semi-dry sparkling wine with strawberries for us, cheese sausage bites as an appetizer, fillet goulash stroganoff with risotto and salad for the main course and coffee and apricot tart for dessert.

That was more than enough. We enjoyed the food and talked about what to do next.

"Maybe everything is half as bad and you'll continue your course at the adult education center," said Hanne, "then maybe we'll meet again in a few days, unless I'm suddenly deported within 24 hours."

"In any case, we'll stay in touch," I replied. "And thank you for offering to help me."

Friday, 25.08.1989: Preparation for the school year 89/90
It was the night before the preparation week. I had gone to bed with depressing thoughts and tossed and turned restlessly until I finally fell into a nightmare in which I was the main character. Amazingly, I could fly. It was nice to float through the air so high up with the sun and look down on the earth. Suddenly, however, the sky darkened and I crashed. Below me was a cemetery. I could look into an excavated grave in which an open coffin stood. I had recognized who the deceased was and got a terrible fright. Cold sweat gathered on my forehead. Fortunately, the alarm clock went off. It was 7.00 am. Relieved, I took a deep breath. No, I hadn't died yet. Nevertheless, the dream gave me food for thought. It wasn't too far removed from reality.

I pushed aside the colorful floral curtains and looked through the window at the cobbled courtyard. "Deceptive tranquillity," I thought.

The children were still asleep. Sandra's second year of apprenticeship didn't start for another week and Frank had to go back to work on Monday. I gulped down an aspirin with some water from the bottle on the bedside cabinet. The thermometer hanging on the window wall outside in the shade showed 24 degrees.

The kitchen smelled of cold cigarette smoke and stale beer. Frank had smoked in the kitchen again and left his pack of diamonds and the full ashtray. I didn't like that. The kitchen only had one window, which was difficult to open. The wooden frame had warped and was stuck. There was also the large baobab plant on the windowsill. I poured the ashes into the garbage can, opened the door to the bathroom and let fresh air in through the bathroom window. The tear-off calendar showed Thursday, 24.08.89. I tore off the page, read it and left it on the kitchen table for Sandra, who had enjoyed reading the back with the sayings since she attended the English course at the adult education center. "Where there's a will, there's a way. Where there is a will, there is a way. William Shakespeare."

The kettle whistled.

I quickly jumped up to take it off the stove so that the children wouldn't wake up. I stumbled over the cat, who was startled into the bathroom and hit my knee on the sharp edge of the table leg. I cried out. That woke Frank up. He stuck his sleepy face through the door: "Is something wrong?" I rubbed my knee: "Not too bad, go back to sleep."

"No, I'm awake now. He took the whistling kettle off the gas. "I'll have a cup of coffee with you and then I want to tinker with my moped a bit."

He brewed two large cups of black coffee and put them on the table. "Milk?" "No, thanks."

"Frank, I don't want to complain, but can't you at least empty the ashtray and put the beer bottles away? You know I can't stand it when it looks and smells like that."

"Okay, okay, now calm down. I know you're nervous about today."

He put bread, jam, cutlery and plates on the table.

"Something to eat?" He grinned.

"Typical," I thought and stroked his shaggy hair. He made an effort to put me at ease. He didn't like it when there were disagreements.

"I've already stopped complaining," I said. "But my nerves really aren't the best at the moment. I don't know what will happen next. I can only assume that I'll be made redundant. Maybe as early as today."

"Wait and see! It could be that nothing happens. You always

worry too much. Back then, when the guy from the Stasi came to school because of my staff work, everything came to nothing."

"When did Sandra actually get home?" I bit into my jam sandwich.

"It wasn't as late as usual. She wants to go camping with Wilfried on the Müritz for another week this morning. That's why he stayed right here."

"It's nice to find out before she's gone."

"My God, we're adults! She still has a week off. She just didn't want to wake you up yesterday."

II felt helpless because there was nothing I could do about it. The children did what they wanted and justified everything by saying they were adults. Fortunately, at least Sandra was on the pill. I didn't want her to end up like me one day, pregnant at 18.

Frank turned the radio to FM and tuned into DT64, the "Morgenrock" program.

"What do you think, Mum?" Tina Turner, the Queen of Rock sang: "What's love got to do with it." He turned the volume up.

"I think it's great, but please turn it down again. I've already taken a headache pill."

He did so wordlessly, then stirred the cup thoughtfully with his spoon. I looked at him.

"Was anyone else here last night?"

"No. Just Sandra and Wilfried. Why?"

"Because of the beer bottles."

"No, we just met a little longer than usual."

Frank took a hearty bite of his thickly smeared jam sandwich.

"And what did you talk about?"

"Oh, various things. Wilfried wants to become FDJ chairman now. He said nobody wants to do it, but maybe you can make a difference in that position. Sandra also thought it was a good idea. Our much-vaunted economy is in a shambles. It would be better to call it a pig economy. Nobody really feels responsible. Everything is rotting away."

"And what did you have in mind? Are you three going to save the state?" I blew on the hot coffee.

"Why not? Everything has to become more sensible. When I was still at school, I didn't know what was going on outside in the factories, but now I can see it for myself every day. When you see the machine parks and material warehouses, you can't help but tear your hair out! All the things that are rotting away! Most of it is still usable material. It's all the people's property, our money, isn't it? It's just thrown away. Nobody cares. The workers prefer to play cards for hours and wait until a delivery comes from somewhere. If there was some kind of switchboard for machines and materials where you could call and the people there would put you in touch with a company where it was lying around, you could just pick it up there and carry on working."

"And what do you do if there is no means of transportation?"

"You can get to grips with that too. There are plenty of old rattletraps that you can get rolling again. There are so many things you could do. But somehow everyone is fed up and nobody changes anything. It's simply unbearable. Something has to be done, right?"

Frank had talked himself into a rage and looked at me in a challenging way.

"You're right, Frank, but it's very difficult in this state to push through anything sensible, you know that yourself. Anyone who criticizes and wants to improve can easily end up on the red list. In general, the party dictates what is right and must be done. You need allies and you have to think carefully about who you say it to and how you say it."

"Mum, if something doesn't change soon, everyone will run away or the borders with Poland and Czechoslovakia will be closed so that no one can leave."

I looked at the clock hanging on the wall above the door.

"I'm sorry. I have to hurry, I haven't even been in the shower. Maybe we can talk more today when I'm back from school."

Frank tossed Mikosch a bottle cap: "Hopp! Catch the mouse!"

I disappeared into the bathroom to take a shower and did a few trunk bends. Then I combed my hair with a wire brush, drew a few lines around my eyes, put on jeans and a T-shirt and was ready. It was almost news time.

"Turn on DDR I, Frank!" The newsreader announced that hundreds of GDR citizens had left the country again and that there was no need to pay attention to people like that.

"Idiot!" Frank remarked and switched off the radio. I picked up my briefcase and walked out of the kitchen door.

"See you later! Hopefully I'll still see Sandra when I get back."

"If you want, you can take the moped!" Frank called after me.

"No thanks, you know very well that I haven't ridden it since you fixed it up!" I heard Frank laugh. Then I got my folding bike out of the garage. The cat didn't miss the chance to follow me through the courtyard door to the corner of the street.

"Go back home, Mikosch," I said. "I have to go to school."

In the School

II rode down the road to the forest and later turned onto the cycle path along the canal. Ten minutes later, I arrived in the neighboring village. The three-storey school complex could be seen from afar. It was still the vacations, but it was the start of my preparation week. I drove down the road to the school, past small detached houses and a queue of people waiting at the bakery. I spotted familiar faces of pupils and villagers. We greeted each other in a friendly manner, as if everything was fine and in a few days everything would be back to normal. A light green Trabi was parked on the street in front of the school. It belonged to Ilse. As I drove past, I noticed that there was a guitar on the back seat. I had a lot to talk to Ilse about the failed trip to Budapest. I parked my bike in the covered bike shed and used the security key to open the large glass door to the school. "I have to pull myself together," I thought. "Maybe Frank is right. Just wait and see." To the left, the stairs led up to the teachers' room, past the chemistry room and the pioneer leader's room.

I opened the door to the staff room.

Laughter rang out to me. People were chatting about their vacation experiences. The atmosphere was relaxed. When Ilse noticed me, she said in an ambiguous tone: "Nice to see you again. I thought you'd gone missing."

"Let's talk about it later," I replied.

The deputy principal had just clapped his hands and asked for silence: "As our comrade principal has been appointed district school inspector at short notice, I would like to welcome you in his place. I'm glad that you're all back safe and sound for the preparation week and that no one has stayed in Hungary."

Everyone laughed except me. I thought I knew that the principal had been appointed to the district school board because of me. I couldn't concentrate. My mind wandered and my gaze lingered on the pictures of Marx and Engels on the opposite wall. "They had also dreamed of a better world," I thought. "But it couldn't be created that quickly." Marx had at least had the chance to emigrate to England back then.

The Communist Party of Great Britain had erected a monument in his honor in Highgate Cemetery in the 1950s, but the world still needed to be changed. The dictatorship of the proletariat was not the last word in wisdom. Those in power had to be controlled, they had to be made to invest more in human thought and the development of common sense. Humanistic education, research, useful work for every individual, regardless of race or class. A good education could perhaps naturally produce a more sensible society in the long term and change the genetic material so that future generations would become more sensitive and just and abolish fanaticism and dictatorships simply because it was below their genetic level. But the first step had not even been taken and only existed in my head.

Next to Marx and Engels hung a picture of Erich Honecker. He smiled rapturously, as if he saw the paradise of communism before him for all eternity, or was looking forward to the big celebration to mark the 40th anniversary of the GDR on October 7. Would he even live to see it? He had been ill for weeks and no longer held the sceptre firmly in his hand, but apparently he didn't want to give it up either. In the background, Egon Krenz, the unloved crown prince, was already preparing to succeed him. But would there ever be freedom to travel in the GDR? The world was open to some, but not to all.

The deputy director concluded his speech: "By the way, our colleague Lehnert has now given birth to a baby boy. We should take up a collection. Will you take over, Comrade

Schmidt?" The pioneer leader nodded.

"All right," the deputy continued, "Take a look at the timetable. If anything else needs to be changed, say it pretty soon. It's very difficult to please everyone anyway. Ilse and I have done a lot of work so that you don't have too many free periods. The new syllabuses and textbooks are on the table next to your subjects. When you've had enough conversation and coffee, you can go home and do your preparations. We'll see you again in a week's time." That was the end of the official part.

"Don't run away!" he called to me, "I still have something to talk to you about." He looked like a giant next to me.

He put his hand on my shoulder and gently pushed me into the headmaster's room where we were alone.

I was sure that he would give me the bad news now. I almost felt sorry for him and I gave him credit for not embarrassing me in front of the whole school. He was actually a nice guy, but he had to do his job. He put me in front of the timetable and kept quiet. I thought he was going to say, "That's all over for you." I felt a shiver run down my spine, even though it was excruciatingly hot in the small unventilated room. He cleared his throat: "Look," he began, and it sounded as if he was searching for the right words in a very awkward situation. I mentally finished his sentence: "I'm so sorry, but after what happened in Berlin, we have to part ways with you."

But instead I heard him say: "We still have a few gaps in the timetable. Ms. Lehnert won't be back until October. Could you temporarily teach military education in year 9?" For a moment, I thought I had to shout out loud. I looked at him dumbfounded.

"What's wrong?" he asked. "Are you having problems with that? You'll manage a bit of marching, explaining the map and compass and putting on bandages, won't you? You get paid extra for it, don't you?"

I hastened to say, "No, no, it's all right", although of course there was a bit more than that to teach, e.g. about biological and chemical weapons and first aid measures. For a moment, I thought about revealing myself to him, telling him everything, asking for understanding and perhaps winning him over as an advocate.

"You're suddenly very pale. Are you not feeling well?" He looked at me scrutinizingly.

"No, everything's fine. Maybe I just need some fresh air."

He opened the window and grinned: "Don't get me pregnant too! The vacations were long enough!"

I tried to smile, but I couldn't quite manage it.

"I didn't sleep most of the night because..."

I made another attempt to explain. But then the phone rang. He made a friendly gesture with his hand and picked up the receiver. I heard him ask: "Who? Our director?"

I left the room. The other colleagues had all left. Ilse had left a note in my seat. "Couldn't wait, have to give guitar lessons now. Please come to my place on Sunday around 3 p.m. and bring your banjo. We can play and chat a bit then. There'll be coffee and cake too."

I put the new curricula and the books for English and military science entitled "Civil Defense Grade 9" in my bag and took a compass and a map of the area from the box in the cupboard for teaching materials. I didn't know how I'd got down the stairs or how I'd managed to get home on my bike. My hands clutched the handlebars trembling. Every time I pedaled, it pounded in my head: "I can't do this anymore. I can't take any more." I knew that this tension would never leave me from now on and that I couldn't live with it. I could feel the fear taking over everything.

Arrival at home

Sandra was no longer at home when I got back from school. She had already gone camping with Wilfried to the Müritz around midday.

Frank was shocked when he saw me sitting at the kitchen table crying: "What's wrong, Mum?" He stood helplessly by and didn't know what to say.

"What's happened?" He stroked my back.

"Nothing, nothing at all. That's just it. I can't stand all this uncertainty. The principal was at the county school board today. Maybe it will happen tomorrow, or the day after tomorrow."

He handed me a paper handkerchief. I blew my nose.

"I got extra lessons today, but when the school year starts, I'll have nothing. I'm finished. They're talking about closing the borders on September 1st. I'll be out of work then. We won't have any money and I don't know what to do next. I'll probably try to fight back. But I also know that I can't win. At some point, I'll probably end up in prison or in a psychiatric ward. That doesn't help any of us."

I looked at my son resolutely: "I have to leave. I have to try, Frank."

He had reservations. "Escape is life-threatening."

"I'll look around and not put myself in danger. If it's not possible, I'll come back.

But if there's an opportunity, I'll take it. If I make it to the West, I will soon find a job and continue to support you financially. I will make sure that we see each other several times a year, perhaps in Prague or Budapest. I promise you that."

I had to think everything through and act as quickly as possible. Frank drove into town with me. We bought a new washing machine and a pair of decent, comfortable running shoes that might help me with a necessary sprint through the border. I had never bought such expensive shoes before. I only left a few marks in the account as it was likely to be confiscated if I didn't return. I could no longer get a map of Hungary in any bookshop. Everything about Hungary was sold out.

I had hardly seen Sandra in the last few weeks and she was on the road again. So I couldn't say goodbye to her. But I wanted to have the feeling that I was always connected to her. Sandra's fingers were the same size as mine. So I went into a jewelry store and bought a pair of friendship rings.

When I came out of the store again, I happened to bump into Gesine with her new boyfriend. 'Hello,' she said, 'nice that we're just meeting. I'd like to invite you for coffee on Sunday. Is it convenient for you?"

I couldn't tell her that this was probably the last time we would meet. Besides, I already had an appointment with Ilse. It wasn't possible to talk about my plans in the presence of the unknown man. But even without him, I probably wouldn't have been able to say anything to Gesine. Too many people were walking past us. So I said: "See you on Sunday then." We gave each other a quick hug and went our separate ways. I hoped Gesine would forgive me one day.

Back home, I settled the most important matters with Frank. We organized the papers, stuck the last loose stamps in the Konsum book so that the Konsum money could be paid out at the beginning of September, and watered the hundred small baobab plants that were to be sold. Then I packed the most necessary things alone in my small rucksack, which was hardly bigger than a school satchel: ID, address book, world receiver, writing materials, laundry, change of clothes.

You had to look neat at a job interview in the West, I thought, and at first I wouldn't have any money to buy anything. So I also added a skirt, blouse, sweater and shoes.

There was a kind of secret compartment at the bottom of the rucksack. That's where I put the remaining forints and the compass that would help me find my way through the border. I stroked our cats for the last time. I would not see my beloved cat Mikosh again. If I managed to escape, I would meet the children somewhere abroad at Christmas.

No, it couldn't be goodbye forever. I knew that my escape plan could be a gamble with my life, but I wouldn't act recklessly. I would simply return home as if nothing had happened. Only if I saw a real chance of getting through would I take it. Sandra thought I was back at Hanne's anyway, helping to bake waffles at the fairground. Frank should let her believe that for the time being so as not to worry her. There was still a week to go before school started and the first of September.

Frank took me to the bus that went to the station. I felt it wasn't right to leave him alone.

I said: "Stick together, you and Sandra. We'll see each other again at Christmas at the latest, in Prague or Budapest."

We hugged each other. He said, "Good luck, mum." I got on the bus and looked after him for as long as I could. It hurt to leave him behind. He became smaller and smaller and finally disappeared from my field of vision. I would never forget this image. It was as if I had left him there at the bus stop and lost him forever.

Chapter IV - Escape

Friday, 25.08.1989 22.00: Berlin-Dresden

I boarded the express train to Dresden in Berlin-Schöneweide. There was no turning back now. The doors closed and the train departed. There were only a few passengers in the compartment I entered. I barely noticed them. They seemed to have become one with the high dark green benches.

Behind the windows of the train was black night. It wasn't worth looking out. In the opposite window, the best I could do was look at my own sad face. I closed my eyes and inwardly said goodbye to the country where I was born and grew up, went to school, studied, got married and had children. For the first time in my life, I had to say goodbye to Frank and Sandra. The mother left the house, not the children, as was customary.

The train jerked and stopped in Elsterwerda. The conductor checked the tickets by marking them on the back of the cardboard with a pencil. Perhaps he suspected what I was up to. Who would travel from Berlin to Geising at night with a rucksack and no return ticket? He gave me a friendly smile and handed me back the ticket. "Here you are. Have a good trip." An elderly couple had boarded and sat down on the opposite bench so that I could hear their conversation. They were worried. Their daughter had not yet returned from her vacation at Lake Balaton with their grandchild. I pretended to be asleep. Maybe I would have talked to them under other circumstances, but the people's conversation triggered my own thoughts about Hungary.

I had got to know a lot about Hungary through Julia. But I couldn't have predicted what I would have to face now. I had to reach Hungary without Julia's help because I no longer had a valid visa. I was on my own and had to cross the green border illegally.

Hungarians didn't have such difficulties. They could travel all over the world without any problems. But GDR citizens were discriminated against everywhere, even in Hungary. In Sopron, I once stood with the children in front of the sign: "GDR citizens stop here". Lake Neusiedl was a restricted zone. It sounded like: Dogs are not allowed in here.

When Julia and her husband visited me once, they spent a day in West Berlin. I took them to the Friedrichstraße S-Bahn station. The journey for GDR citizens ended here. On their return, Julia gave me a postcard of West Berlin because she knew that I collected postcards. Julia told me what they had seen: the Victory Column, Charlottenburg Palace, Kaufhaus des Westens and even the back of the Brandenburg Gate and the Wall from the Kudamm.

Julia had told me that her eldest daughter was planning to go to London to study music and learn the English language. That was now possible for the Hungarians.

One of my mother's cousins, Willi Sokolowsky, lived in London. He had married an English woman after the war. When my mother was still alive, he often visited us. But because she lived in the GDR, she was of course not allowed to visit him. The comparison between Hungary and the GDR didn't help me now, of course. It only fueled my hatred of the constant discrimination and the thought of finally having to free myself from it.

In the afternoon, when I was in the city with Frank, I had seen more drunks than ever before, which made me think of the words of my old German teacher: "When a social order declines, the first sign is the decline of customs and traditions." The mood of doom could be felt everywhere. It was time for something new to begin. Could Michael Gorbachev implement his ideas of glasnost[32] and perestroika?[33] Was there hope for openness and transformation, hope that I would one day be able to live out my wanderlust? I didn't just want to see on postcards where others had been.

I wrote letters to the world that was closed to me. I tried to bring the world home, to absorb something of the breath of the unknown. Nigeria, the Sahel, the tropical rainforest with its exotic plants and wild animals, the colorful clothes of the different tribes, the fishing boats on the Niger and in the middle of it all, there was one person who was more familiar to me than anyone else. He was just as Mr. Winkler had described him, a valuable person. Sometimes I thought that life was not worth living without him. I lived with him in my thoughts all those years, even when my lovers changed. I always remained true to his soul. I sent my thoughts to him and he comforted me, stood by me. He was my dream man, who would always remain a dream, because it wasn't friendship or love that would win out, but socialism.

I looked out into the darkness. The train rattled monotonously past small towns with hardly any lights on. The conductor opened the compartment door with a loud clatter. I turned to face him. He punched a hole in the piece of cardboard and disappeared into the next carriage with the door crashing open again.

A few seats further on, a young mother was trying to calm her crying baby. Next to her sat a lanky young man, who was probably the father, talking soothingly to the baby. A large rucksack stood in the square opposite. Perhaps they had the same intention as me. Somehow the woman looked a bit like

32 transparency
33 restructuring

114

Sandra. How would Sandra take my departure? At the moment it seemed as if she was fixated on Wilfried, her boyfriend, for all eternity. They were making plans for the future, wanted to study in Berlin, get married, have children. Like the couple sitting there on the train? Would Sandra miss me very much or see my departure as completely natural? The children were now experiencing what separation means for the first time with the departure of their mother. I, on the other hand, had already experienced many separations as a small child. My closest relatives had always defected to the class enemy and allowed themselves to be seduced by capitalism. By the time the Wall was built, almost half of my relatives had fled to the western part of Germany, mostly via Berlin, lived for a while in the Gießen or Friedland reception camps and finally started a new life in which their eastern relatives no longer had any part. They settled in Stuttgart, Munich, Hanover, Bremen and Aschaffenburg. One cousin died for the Foreign Legion, another was found hanged from a tree somewhere near Hamelin, next to his car. His case was never solved.

People who were not related to the West had it easier. They didn't know these inner conflicts. Many followed the guidelines of ideology. Their truth was the truth of those in power. Socialism was the path on which they progressed in a straight line. Marxism-Leninism became their religion. They did not think about whether Marx might have been wrong.

The division of Germany brought with it much suffering and grief. But people hardly talked about it among themselves. They endured this silent suffering. It was part of life, like everything else that governments or rulers imposed on their people. You had to accept what could not be changed and always make the best of it, because after all, you still had to live. That has always been the case.

The steady rattling of the train made me doze off for a short while. But one of the train windows didn't close properly and a cold breeze blew through the compartment, making me freeze and waking me up again and again as soon as I fell asleep. I took my sweater out of my rucksack and covered my knees with it.

Preparation for possible border control issues

I wanted to take the train from Dresden to Altenberg in the morning and get off in Geising, the last town before the Czechoslovakian border. Then I would walk to the Zinnwald border crossing. I played through situations and questions at the border in my mind. I already knew that it wouldn't be easy, that everything depended on how thoroughly I was prepared and whether I kept my nerve. I only had this one chance to give my life a new direction. "Where there's a will, there's a way" had been written on the tear-off calendar. That was now my guiding principle. It gave me the security I needed to start what I wanted to finish. Everything depended on me alone. I tried to imagine my situation in Zinnwald. The customs officers would look at my identity card and see that I had already been to Hungary once this year. That could be an advantage. After all, I could have stayed in Hungary like thousands of others. But I had come back. My visa had now expired. Who would have thought that I was planning to cross the green border into Hungary now? There were about 600 km between Zinnwald and Hungary. So why wouldn't anyone believe that I just wanted to take a short hike to Teplice in the last few days of my vacation so that I could be rested and ready to face my school class again in a few days' time?

It was possible that the border guards wouldn't let me

through because my name was already on a list. But I didn't even want to think about that. If I was searched, they might ask where my return ticket to Berlin was. I would answer that I had only bought a one-way ticket because I was going back from Teplice in my friends' car. We wanted to do something together and then drive back to Berlin via Görlitz.

I also thought about what else I might have said to the fictitious friends, what their names were, where they lived and what type of car they owned. The story had to be simple and comprehensible.

It wasn't the first time I'd had to slip into a role that demanded a convincing acting performance. But I was the kind of actor who struggles with stage fright. I needed enough time to adjust to stressful situations. Only when I was completely calm inside did I manage to deliver the text convincingly. I also had to learn early on that lying was sometimes necessary to protect myself and others.

I had had to grow up with the schizophrenia of divided thinking that the division of Germany brought with it.

It was not a pleasant situation to have to live with an official and a private opinion, but if you understood the rules of the game, they made life easier. All you had to do was react convincingly and you could successfully slip through the cracks. Nevertheless, I never managed to acquire a "thick skin". On the contrary, my sensitivity grew. I paid attention to every possible ambiguity in words so that I could stay out of things and was always on my guard against particularly good friends.

Saturday, August 26, 6.00 a.m.: From Geising to Zinnwald
I arrived in Geising, the last German town before the Czech border, at around six o'clock in the morning, overtired and frozen through. Only a few fellow travelers got off the train. Among them was the young family with the baby. Everyone left the small station building so quickly that I thought the dawn had swallowed them up. I was the only one left and continued under the trees along the long village road, which soon led to the 3 km long basalt-stone road through the middle of the forest to Zinnwald.

I had been here once before on vacation with the children, we had hiked a lot, climbed the over 800 m high Geisingberg and looked down on the mountains and valleys from the Lousienturm. I could remember that the conifers on the hill-tops looked bare and yellowish, especially on the heights between Zinnwald and Teplice. There was obvious environmental damage caused by Czech industry.

The children and I had also taken a bus to Teplice and visited the beautiful spa town with its medieval houses and baroque castle, where Beethoven, Goethe, Chopin and Liszt had all stayed. The children had enjoyed the flea market the most. But none of that mattered now. The only thing that mattered to me was that I knew the area and had a rough idea of my escape route. I wanted to take a train from Teplice to Bratislava. The Hungarian border was then not far away. Maybe I would swim across the Danube. But I had to decide that on the spot. I had no idea how the border between Czechoslovakia and Hungary was secured. All I knew was that there was no barbed wire or mines on the German-Polish border, the "Oder-Neisse peace border". It was probably similar between Czechoslovakia and Hungary. There were only mine paths on the borders with the capitalist countries.

I walked quickly through the forest. The cool morning air stung my face like a thousand fine needles. Tears welled up in my eyes. I wiped them away with the sleeve of my rain jacket. Apart from the birdsong in the morning, there was no sound to be heard, not even the crack of a twig, no car, no bicycle overtook me. Everything seemed unreal, like in a dream.

The dark blue pavement of the street suddenly reminded me of the street where I went to school as a child, and for a brief moment I felt transported back to my childhood. Full of gratitude, I thought back to my parents, who had sadly been gone for a long time. I had the feeling that they were suddenly with me and would stand by me, just as they always had. This thought calmed me down. I looked up at the patch of sky that the forest aisle revealed and I knew that I was not alone. They lived in my thoughts and they would be with me on the way into the unknown, if only for the sake of their grandchildren. They would give me the strength to get through everything and make sure that I saw my children again soon. I explained to my parents that I was leaving so that I could continue to look after Sandra and Frank, I hadn't left my children. And my parents understood me and gave me strength and courage.

Zinnwald, Border crossing

The closer I got to the open area in front of the border crossing, the more uncertain I became. In my current state, it wasn't advisable to head straight for the border checkpoint.

I had to think about everything again.

At the checkpoint, two customs officers were standing behind a barrier and talking. There were no passers-by to be seen. I had assumed there would be a lot of people. But I was apparently the only one who wanted to cross the border here. I realized that I was going to be thoroughly searched and questioned. On the outside I probably looked tired or indifferent, but in reality I was very excited, my heart was racing. At some distance from the customs officers, I turned right and headed straight for the wooden beam house, which was a restaurant.

There were only a few people in the restaurant. Over a cup of coffee at a high table in the warm room, I thought again about the possible situations that could come my way, thought through the questions and answers and realized that I was slowly becoming calmer. I had made up my mind and wanted to get it over with now. When I looked at my watch, it was exactly 08:00. I left the restaurant.

There was still no one to be seen at the control booth. I pushed my ID card through the small window. The customs officer slowly leafed through all the pages and looked at every single Hungarian visa in detail. I made a friendly face as if my best friend was behind the glass and even managed to strike up a trivial conversation about the really good hiking weather. However, I was not released so easily. I was asked to come with them to a small wooden hut. There I was thoroughly patted down by another officer and had to empty my jacket and trouser pockets. I was asked where I was coming from, where I was going, where I worked, why I didn't have a return ticket, how I was getting home again, etc. I was well prepared for the answers. I had to empty my rucksack. On the table were: washing kit, writing materials, address book, world receiver, change of clothes, skirt, sweater, a pair of pumps and a wallet. In the wallet were Czech crowns, a few GDR marks and pictures of my children. I didn't open the secret pocket with the compass and the Hungarian forints.

The officer didn't notice them.

Not everyone was allowed to cross the border now. Too many had already found ways through the green border to Hungary. Those who were caught were sent to prison for a few years.

I had to wait in the checkpoint for almost an hour. I had the feeling that the walls were watching me. It was similar to the Honecker consultation a few weeks ago. They could make me sit there at will and show me that they would not tolerate any dissent. I despised these methods, but I also knew that there was no way of resisting them. If you didn't want to be broken, you had to try to outwit the system and escape. So I played the role of the annoyed person in the bus shelter who finally wanted to leave. I looked at my watch and silently said to myself: "My God, does it have to take so long?" I suppressed my real thoughts. If I was being watched, I had to play my part well.

The customs officer who had patted me down finally opened the door and led me outside. I still had to wait in front of the counter of another control house, behind the window of which a uniformed man was making a very concentrated phone call. Perhaps he was calling my school to make sure everything was correct. I continued to act bored and friendly. In reality, I could barely contain my thoughts. Maybe they wouldn't let me leave the country.

Finally, the uniformed man behind the counter looked at me kindly, pressed the "Zinnwald, GDR" stamp into my ID card and handed it back to me through a flap in the window.

"Well then, have a nice day!" I could hardly believe it, pocketed the ID card and forced myself to leave the GDR at a normal pace. Three officers, who were much younger than me, looked after me.

On Czech soil

On Czech soil, I met people with children whose laughter reassured me.

They were returning from vacation and hurrying to get home, where their parents or grandparents were already looking after them. I walked quickly along the valley road to Teplice, which was surrounded by the mountains of the Ore Mountains. I came across a few scattered Trabants and a Skoda. Since I had last been here in the Ore Mountains, the pollution had increased even further. The trees on the heights were particularly badly damaged. Once magnificent green spruce and fir trees not only looked yellow and brown, but many had dried up and died. Some were reminiscent of upright, burnt matches that could snap at any moment. Deciduous trees stretched their dead gray branches towards the sky like memorials.

It was quiet all around, but the earth was slowly awakening in the morning sun that had broken through the cloud cover. Surrounded by the diverse buzzing of insects, I walked along the road at a steady pace. The parched yellow grass at the side of the road crunched under my feet. I had the impression that I was walking through an endless steppe.

The sun quickly warmed up the air and the land and lay on my shoulders, which felt good after the long, cool night. It smelled of hay. A few cars drove past. I made no effort to stop them. It was better to rely only on myself.

I took the world receiver out of my rucksack and turned on the Austrian radio. It was reported that there were Stasi people at the border with Hungary intercepting the fugitives and that thousands of refugees were already in Hungarian reception camps hoping for a decision from the West German government to allow them to enter West Germany.

From Teplice to Bratislava

By now it was lunchtime. I had already been on the road for three hours and could already see the turn-off to Teplice on the right-hand side. Then I noticed two trucks with Romanian license plates in a parking lot. The two truck drivers were sitting on folding stools eating a meal as I passed by.

They shouted something at me that I didn't understand, but it sounded like a question. I paused. They gave me a friendly nod and I wondered if they could take me with them. If they were going to Romania, they would have to drive through Hungary. I spoke to them in German and English. But they didn't understand me. As they seemed to be my age, they must have learned Russian at school. But they couldn't communicate in Russian either. In the end, I tried with my hands and feet, showed my ID with the Hungarian visa and made it clear to them that I wanted to go to Hungary illegally. The truck drivers, who had come from Dresden, agreed to give me a lift. I had no reservations, especially as they were driving two trucks in a row. I abandoned the plan to take the train from Teplice to Bratislava. I could probably reach the Hungarian border area much more quickly and safely and save a bit of money. I got in with the truck driver who was following behind.

The journey on the transit route through Czechoslovakia took the whole day. We stopped several times. The two men had boiled water on a small alcohol stove and brewed peppermint tea in rather dented aluminum cups. They had also handed me a cup of tea, which I drank out of politeness but with reluctance.

The landscape they were driving through wasn't particularly interesting, flat land, fields, gray towns. Perhaps I was also too tired to take it all in. I had to concentrate on the essentials.

After all, this trip was not a vacation. We drove a long way around Prague, then towards Brno and finally towards Bratislava. I hadn't thought that the journey would take so long and be so exhausting. The truck driver I was riding with looked at me more and more often in a way that made me uncomfortable. He brushed his stringy hair out of his face, winked at me and kept whispering something to me that I couldn't understand but was unmistakable. I tried to ignore the situation by looking out of the window and keeping as little eye contact as possible. I didn't want to give him any reason to even remotely think that I was going to have sex with him just because he had taken me. I caught a whiff of his sweat and smoke and felt disgusted just thinking about it. His big belly was bulging out from under his much too short T-shirt. I pretended to be asleep. Suddenly I felt his right hand on my thigh. He was only holding the steering wheel with his left hand. I indicated to him that I didn't want that and moved away from him as far as I could.

It was already dark outside. I thought about how I could escape the situation that was inexorably approaching. We had been on the road for more than 10 hours and would soon be stopping to spend the night in a parking lot. Nothing could happen to me while we were driving, but as soon as the truck stopped. I tried to take his mind off things and handed him the pictures of my children. I wanted to remind him of his family, which he probably had. He handed the pictures back to me without really looking at them. We drove through a huge wooded area. I could read a sign in the headlights. We were near Bratislava.

Sunday, 27.08.1989: In the forest of Bratislava

It was just after midnight. The date on the clock now showed August 27th. Both trucks stopped in a parking lot high in the woods near Bratislava, where several other vehicles were already parked. The truck driver smiled at me and mumbled something incomprehensible. I was glad when his colleague opened the door from the outside. I picked up my rucksack and made it clear that I was in a hurry but would be right back. I made my way into the bushes.

The darkness was not pleasant, but I also knew that the night could offer me protection.

From a distance, I could see the large parking lot. I wasn't sure if the two drivers would come looking for me. So I went deeper into the forest, leaned against a tree trunk and sat on my rucksack to get some sleep. However, it was freezing cold and I realized that sleep was out of the question. I had to move around to avoid freezing to death. The night in the densely forested mountains was starry. I walked in a wide arc through the forest, stepped out of the darkness and made my way along the downhill road. Although I must have been completely tired because I hadn't slept for the second day, I was wide awake and listened to every sound, no matter how quiet.

I kept walking as fast as I could to keep warm. As soon as I noticed a headlight, I lay flat in the ditch or hid behind a bush. When there was a sudden loud crack around a bend, I was so startled that I stopped, paralyzed. A large figure was lurking in the bushes with the moon shining on it. I didn't dare go any further, I was completely defenseless and waited for a bad end. Suddenly, however, branches whizzed through the air. I held on to the crash barrier. A huge deer jumped out of the bushes right in front of me and vanished into the darkness of the forest on the other side of the road. When the seconds of fright were over, I armed myself with a sturdy, not too heavy branch so that I could defend myself in an emergency. But I probably didn't need to be afraid at all here in the dark forest. Animals wouldn't hurt me. The deer had probably even been frightened by me. And who was to know that I was walking alone here?

The long-lost instincts of primitive man seemed to awaken in me again and functioned reliably. Extremely focused, all my senses switched on, I continued walking, solely concerned with making as little noise as possible and taking in every sound around me in order to be able to cope with a dangerous situation. Fortunately, the soles of my shoes were very soft. If there was a crack in the undergrowth, I held my breath, stopped, listened and stood ready to defend myself. After a few hours, I felt that my behavior was completely normal. I walked down the road all night long. Before the sun rose again, the first birds began to chirp sporadically. As time went on, the bird calls became louder and more varied. A woodpecker knocked somewhere nearby. As the light increased, so did the traffic on the transit road. I was no longer hiding. It was unlikely that anyone would ambush me now. Too many cars were passing by.

Fortunately, I could soon make out a town in the distance, but it seemed more like a mirage. It was still so far away and seemed to float in the air. Maybe I still had further to go, until the evening. This thought and my exhaustion made me despondent for a while. Suddenly, a truck with German license plates pulled up next to me. The driver was from Passau. He spoke to me with a Turkish accent. I was skeptical. He had a friendly face, but so had the others. I didn't want to put myself in danger again. But should I never trust anyone again? I didn't think the man was dangerous and, as I had certainly run more than one marathon, I got in after all. I told him what had happened to me and what I was planning to do. The driver said I didn't need to be afraid. He wouldn't mind being with such a beautiful woman... but only if I wanted to. I already regretted getting in the car. Couldn't any man accept that I would go to such lengths to become a free man? Did every man believe that a woman traveling alone with a rucksack on her back was only out for adventure and was eagerly waiting to be raped and humiliated? I brought the conversation back to the real issue. He handed me his car atlas and I was able to get my bearings as to where we were. We were driving through the border triangle, Hungary, Austria and Czechoslovakia. "Austria is not far from here. Less than 40 km to Vienna. But you can't get through. It's not like Hungary. The road is mined from here," said the driver. How easy it could have been. I was in a West German truck from Passau. The driver lived there. But I had to try to cross the borders of Slovakia and then the borders of Hungary to get to Austria and then to Germany. The truck driver said: "The Danube is not far from here. It flows through a divided city, called Komarno in Slovak and Komarom in Hungarian." I looked at the area ahead of us on the map. Maybe there was a good chance here and I could swim across the Danube. He couldn't take me any further. The driver stopped one place before the Hungarian border crossing at Rajka and let me out. The place was called Samorin and was right on the Danube and the border with Hungary. I now had to find the loophole in the green border all by myself.

Slovakian border region, Samorin

In Samorin, I walked along a cobbled village street that ran in a curve and was relatively wide compared to other streets. On the left-hand side of the road, a long gray wall stretched into the village, behind which stood fruit trees. Simple but well-kept-looking houses adjoined it. On the right-hand side, there was a bus stop with a glass roof, where a few men and women were waiting with shopping bags. I approached a woman about my age. She was carrying a basket with fresh bread in it. It smelled very tempting and for a moment I wasn't sure whether I would take the bread from the woman and just bite into it. I was really hungry. My stomach started growling loudly. But I pulled myself together. Attempts to speak to the woman in German or English were unsuccessful. It worked with Hungarian. "Hol van pék?"[34]

I was able to follow her explanations, which she supported with gestures, to some extent and was able to recognize the bakery store, which was not far from the bus stop on the other side of the street. Since I still had a few crowns, I went there and bought a whole loaf of kenyér.[35] I tore off a large piece and devoured it ravenously. The rest went into my rucksack. I walked back to the bus stop. A few minutes later, a bus labeled Komarno stopped. I bought a ticket, sat down on a free seat and fell asleep from sheer exhaustion, surrounded by a babble of voices in Slovakian and Hungarian. I hadn't been able to prepare for this journey and knew next to nothing about this region. I hadn't even expected that most people here spoke Hungarian. But wars have repeatedly changed the borders for thousands of years and the population has been ruthlessly torn apart. Before the Second World War,

34 Where is the baker?
35 bread

128

this part of the country had belonged to Hungary, but now the ethnic Hungarians were the largest part of the population, but they lived in Czechoslovakia.

At the terminus, one of the older men who had been standing at the bus stop in Samorin woke me up. He gently tapped me on the shoulder and said a few words that I didn't understand, probably in Slovakian. For a moment I felt safe. He looked like a nice grandpa in his light-colored shirt and dark pants held up by suspenders. We smiled at each other. Then we each went our separate ways.

Komarno

From the bus station I walked down a very long straight road that led to the Danube, always careful to recognize possible Stasi people early on. The world receiver had told me again that there were many GDR refugees at the borders and that inconspicuous Stasi people were trying to track them down to bring them back. I had to try not to stand out and not draw attention to myself. In those days, a rucksack on my back was suspicious. Luckily, my rucksack was small. I held it in my hand like a shopping bag. To give myself the appearance of taking a quiet stroll through the city, I stopped in front of a store from time to time. Bathing equipment was on display in a shop window, including a swimming ring. Maybe I could swim across the Danube at night with its help. The store wouldn't open for a few minutes. I wanted to think about it and maybe come back.

When I arrived on the banks of the Danube, I couldn't believe my eyes. A large fortress rose up just a few meters away from me, on the other bank. It reminded me of Buda Castle. A small ferry with a few people was just crossing over there. I could clearly see border guards checking passports. I didn't

129

know what would happen if I was checked. So it was better if I got out of here as quickly as possible. But if I left abruptly and quickly, I might have given myself away. So I walked along the banks of the Danube for a while as if it were a matter of course. Everyone could only be convinced that I was from Komarno. My act was so bold that it simply had to be believable. Nevertheless, I looked around carefully. The first thing I noticed was a huge searchlight that would circle its light wheel over the Danube at night. I gave up the idea of swimming across the Danube with a swimming ring disguised as a pile of brushwood.

I had to think of something else. I was overcome by tiredness. I walked back down the long street to the station. I read the name Ferenc Lehar on a half-torn poster on the advertising pillar and looked at the composer's portrait for a while. The poster probably announced a concert. But that wasn't why I had come here. My only thought was to go to sleep some-where. I had to find a bench. But I couldn't find one. At the store with the swimming ring, I bought a postcard with a stamp. I absolutely had to write a message to my children. It started to drizzle. I looked for a place to take shelter. The train station was nearby. There was also a post box there. On the station forecourt, under a tree, stood a young man (Sinti or Roma) who had laid out watches on a small table in front of him. He tried to sell them as I walked past. As there was no one else around, I spoke to him in Hungarian and asked if he knew a way to Hungary where there were no checks. He laughed and said yes.

I would have to come home with him. He made a clear gesture with his hand. I got annoyed and left him standing there. He shouted something after me and laughed.

The station concourse looked empty and dingy. There was

crumpled paper, old tickets and leftover food lying around. There were a few old dark brown wooden benches in the middle of the room. There was a counter on the right and a small store on the left where you could buy something. A woman in long colorful dresses stood at the counter with her two children and talked to the salesman. I sat down on the bench and wrote the card to my children. "Don't worry about anything. Everything will be fine. See you later. Best wishes from Komarno". They knew my handwriting and didn't need a sender's name, which might have been an advantage, because I was probably already registered with the Stasi. In the meantime, it was pouring outside. I put the card in the letterbox and went back into the station building. A timetable for the regional train from Komarno via Nove Zamky to Sahy was hanging in a glass case. Just as I was about to take a closer look at the timetable and the route, the woman with the children came up to me. First she begged for some money, then for some food, then for cigarettes. I had nothing I could give her except two lumps of sugar that I still had in my jacket pocket from the coffee in Zinnwald. I gave them to the children, who immediately put them in their mouths and ran through the hall screaming loudly. The woman didn't leave my side. I needed some sleep and was afraid that my few things might be stolen. I went to the toilet, closed the door behind me and fell asleep on the toilet seat. I must have slept there for half an hour when a loudspeaker voice announced that the train from Budapest to Berlin was arriving. Should I just get on and go home again? It looked like I wasn't going to make it. I was tired and completely exhausted. It was just too dangerous to cross the border as a woman alone. In order to be able to sleep for at least a few minutes and not be robbed of my last belongings, I had had to save myself in a stinking station toilet, like a drug addict or bum. I was frustrated. The biggest danger wasn't even the customs officers, the border guards or the Stasi people who were supposedly in the border areas to track down fugitives. I could prepare myself for that. The worst thing was having to confide in people you didn't know because you were dependent on their help, because you had to ask for directions or where to go shopping. And you didn't know what they thought of you. Men in particular tried to take advantage of my helpless situation. That was a realization that shocked me and that I hadn't expected. I had voluntarily and naively walked into a dangerous maze, convinced that I would find my destination. But it took more than geographical knowledge. In this maze, I was worthless and without rights, fair game running around. I could be exploited, abused or even killed. Who would care? It was only thanks to my intuition that I had been able to escape from the Bratislava forest in time before anything happened. It wasn't the darkness and the wild animals that had been the worst thing, but the fear that the men were chasing me and could still catch up. I had run for my life, developed powers I had never known before and had been glad when I finally arrived in a town where people went about their normal lives and nobody was interested in me. I had resolved not to ask anyone, to behave inconspicuously like a local and to deal with everything myself. If I wanted to start a new life, I had to avoid any risks.

After the loudspeaker announcement, the station concourse filled up with travelers. Some of them were already waiting for someone. Joyful reunions, children's cries and unintelligible shouts rang through the wide waiting hall.

I let the train from Budapest to Berlin depart. Trains to Berlin ran frequently from here. I didn't want to give up in a hurry and give myself one last chance.

The monotonous babble of voices, of which I understood nothing, had a soporific effect. I wrapped the strap of my rucksack around my arm so that it couldn't be stolen. I closed my eyes and found myself in a strange waking-sleeping state. My mind said goodbye and handed over its task to my subconscious, which paid close attention to every unknown, unusual noise. But nothing unusual happened around me and I almost fell asleep. But then I suddenly heard my mother tongue close to me.

Acquaintance with two men from the GDR

Two young men, maybe in their mid-20s, were talking. When I was sure that they were in the same situation as me, I jumped up, stood next to them and asked: "Are you from the GDR?" They laughed and the taller of the two said: "Yes, but not for long." I knew immediately that I had found allies. Stasi spies didn't look like these guys, with old worn-out sandals and clothes that you could tell hadn't just been put on this morning. They had rucksacks on and looked a bit tired.

"I have a compass," I said.

I had just wanted to give up. And then suddenly everything changed. I knew immediately that, together with these young men, I could escape. We had a common goal: to win our freedom.

The younger of the two told me: "We should forget about the Danube, it's too dangerous. Tonight they caught our friend here in Komarno. He had put undergrowth on his head and tried to swim across the Danube. We had both warned him. But he didn't listen to us. The searchlights lit up the whole area. They simply fished him out and took him away. We saw it from a distance and made sure we got away."

The taller one added, barely audible: "He'll probably have to serve five years for this." He lowered his eyes and shrugged his shoulders helplessly. The silence of a minute's silence spread. I sensed that he was infinitely sorry. Then he wiped his face with his sleeve and said firmly:

"But we still don't want to go back."

I could imagine exactly what had happened. I had seen the searchlight on the banks of the Danube.

"Maybe we can make it through the woods with the compass," I said.

"Do you know how to use it?"

"Well, I'm supposed to be teaching military education in year 9 from next week."

"Oh, a teacher wants to run away?" I sensed an undertone in his voice that I didn't like and replied: "It doesn't matter now, does it? My name is Isa, by the way, and I have two children your age at home."

The two of them laughed: "You expect us to believe that?" I showed them my ID.

"That's right! Then we'll call you Aunt Isa, won't we? "

"You're making fun of me, aren't you?" Now I had to laugh too.

"And what's your name?

"That's Jörg," said the shorter one.

"And this one is Christian," said the tall one.

"Great, then we can be on a first-name basis and call each other by name from now on." A spark of sympathy had been ignited. We were in the same boat.

"Come with me," I said. "I saw a map of the area around Komarno over there. Maybe that will help us."

We took a long look at the course of the railroad line, which made a large curve to the northwest towards Nove Zamky and then led east along the Hron River back to the border area to Sturovo on the Danube. On the opposite bank was the Hungarian town of Esztergom.

I said: "We don't have a map, but a compass should be enough. We know where north is and we're following a certain number pointing east. That will get us to Hungary."

We decided to avoid the Danube and look for the most difficult escape route, which was probably also the safest. To do this, we had to go further north. There might be a few smaller rivers there, but none would be as big as the Danube. We agreed to try Sahy first and explore our chances there.

Sunday, August 27, 1989, 3 p.m.: Komarno to Nove Zamky

I went to the counter to buy three tickets to Sahy: "Három jegyet Sahyre, kérem." I could only guess what the woman behind the counter was asking. But she could only have meant: "There and back?"

"Nem vissza"[36], I said hastily. Jörg and Christian were amazed at my language skills. I led them to believe that I was almost perfect. In reality, after all these years, I had only just learned a few tourist phrases. The tickets together cost 27 Czech crowns, almost a quarter of the money I still had. The woman at the counter was very friendly and wrote down the transfer stations and departure times on a piece of paper. The train connection went from Komárno via Nóve Zámky (Neuhäusel), Stúrovo and Cata to Sahy. The train departed at around 16:00 and was scheduled to arrive in Sahy at 20:39. We had to decide on the spot whether Sahy was the place from which we would attempt to cross the border. In any case, we would stay in Czechoslovakia until we had found

---

36 not back

135

the most suitable place, even if it took a whole week.

Soon after the train left Komárno, we crossed the Váh (Waag), the longest river in Czechoslovakia, which flows into the Danube in Komarno, on the railroad bridge. We continued through a small wooded area, after which the landscape became more open, with fields of grain, green meadows and groups of trees. It looked like a fertile agricultural area. Every now and then a small settlement or a pond could be seen. But the sky was gray. It was raining away. Drops collected on the train windows and slowly trickled down. The train only stopped in a few places and was almost empty. The seats were made of wood and not very comfortable, but we were glad to be in the dry. "Why do you actually want to leave the GDR?" I asked.

Christian, who was cleaning his glasses, replied: "I've applied to leave the country. My grandfather in Hanover died a few months ago and left behind an electrical workshop. I could take it over. I trained as an electrician, along with Jörg and Tom, by the way, who they caught." Jörg nodded, leaned into a corner and tried to sleep.

Christian said: "It's probably the best thing we can do. Just take a nap. Who knows what's in store for us today. You have to make the most of every opportunity. I'm also dog-tired. We've been on the road for a week and have always slept somewhere outdoors."

"Did you apply for a visa?"

"No, we wouldn't have got it anyway, if only because of the application to leave the country. We got here by hitchhiking and on foot."

"All right, we really should get some rest."

I leaned my head against my rucksack and tried to sleep. When you haven't been able to sleep in for days, it was easy to nod off at every opportunity. I was glad that I was no longer alone and didn't have to worry about being robbed. Once the conductor checked the tickets. He punched holes in the brown cardboard tickets.

After an hour we arrived at Nóve Zámky station. I had the feeling of arriving at a huge steelworks. All I could see from the platform were rails, tracks, container trains, halls and a shunting yard. In the background were a few blocks of flats, similar to the new housing estates in the GDR. Nóve Zámky must have been a medium-sized industrial town. Everything looked gray. The air smelled of chemicals and exhaust fumes. I wouldn't have time to get to know the town any other way. Maybe there were sights here, similar to Komarno. Probably all these towns in the border region had an interesting historical core, fortresses, castles, defenses, I thought. The people who lived here had not found peace for thousands of years. There had always been occupiers and border disputes in this area. The Romans were here, the Mongols, the Magyars, the Ottomans, the Habsburgs, the Nazis.

We had to change trains to catch the connecting train via Sturovo to Sahy.

A few locals were also waiting on the platform.

I categorized most of them as Sinti and Roma.

As it was cold and wet, we were glad when the train to Sturovo was announced and we were able to get back on.

Sturovo

The train returned to the border area along the Hron River to Sturovo. Here we had to be particularly careful again, keep a close but unobtrusive eye on our surroundings and, above all, avoid talking to each other when people were nearby. Christian and Jörg could easily have passed for Slovaks or

Hungarians. They looked tanned and had dark hair. Their clothes were no different from those worn by the locals, except perhaps Jörg's sandals. Christian said: "I think they're the sloppiest things I've ever seen." Jörg just waved them off: "The main thing is to be comfortable!" With my light skin color and blond hair, it was easy to suspect that I was a stranger in these parts. However, it was the men's rucksacks with the sleeping mats that stood out the most.

As the train pulled into Sturovo, I thought I was dreaming. The Danube lay close in front of us and on the other bank, on a hill surrounded by vineyards, rose a monumental building, the castle of Esztergom with the huge round dome of the basilica. It was only a few hundred meters to Hungary. How easy it would have been to paddle across by boat. But there was no way to reach Hungary that way. On the contrary, we had to stay away from the Danube. A few young people who had also got off the train suddenly joined us and took photos. I was approached by a young man in German: "This is the largest church in Hungary. Impressive, isn't it?" I looked at him, smiled and replied: "Nincs értem." (I don't understand). (I don't understand.) He seemed puzzled, smiled too and went back into the station building. We had half an hour to wait before continuing our journey. "I didn't have a good feeling. Christian also said: "We shouldn't wait in the station building. Let's take a walk outside until we can continue our journey."

Tupá

After boarding the train to Sahy in Sturovo, we decided to get off in Tupá, a village before Sahy.

It seemed safer than arriving at the station in the border town and possibly being stopped there. It was already very dark and there was no moon or stars in the sky. There were two roads leading out of the town from the station, a busier one with lots of cars and a quieter one on the left along a row of detached and semi-detached houses. There had to be a small wood on the right-hand side of the road. Maybe it was just a few dense groups of trees. It was impossible to tell exactly. In addition to the darkness, there was fog and an unpleasant drizzle. We could hardly see a hand in front of our eyes. It was only because a few cars came towards us that we could see anything at all of the surroundings. Every now and then we had to jump onto the grass verge. It was life-threatening. The cars drove past us too close and too fast. We could no longer see anything and had no idea how far it was to Sahy. I suggested that we should soon find somewhere to spend the night. There was suddenly a terrible smell of ash and garbage in the air. There must be a landfill nearby. The road continued straight ahead, but we decided to take a path that led slightly downhill to the right into a small wood. We stumbled through the darkness, followed by the stench of the landfill.

The trees soon thinned out and ended at a small river with a wide grassy bank.

"Maybe the border is already beyond the river," said Jörg.

"Could be, but we'll have to explore it in daylight."

We walked along the shore for a while until we had escaped the stench.

"Let's stay here," I said.

We wondered a little as we looked around.

"It's almost like a campsite."

"Isn't there a tent there?

"Indeed there is."

"Maybe there are people inside."

"Maybe some who want to leave too."

"Who knows."

We approached cautiously. There was nothing to hear, no snoring, no movement.

"If we want to know if someone is in there, we should throw a stone or something at the tent. It usually scares you and makes a noise," said Jörg.

He threw a stone and Christian threw another one. But everything remained silent. "I hope there isn't a body in there," said Jörg.

"Let's go a little way away from the tent and sleep somewhere here," I said.

The men lay down on their sleeping mats and soon fell asleep.

I heard them snoring. It had stopped raining, but it was dripping from the trees and making unfamiliar noises. I sat down on my rucksack and leaned against a tree, listening for every drip and crackle. A little owl cried in the distance. The cold of the ground crept into my body. I nodded off but kept waking up, shivering from the cold, chattering my teeth, walking back and forth a few steps and rubbing my thighs to stop the pins and needles. I envied the men who slept easily. There seemed to be no end to the night.

Monday, 28.08.1989: At the river Ipel

The sun rose at around 5.00 am. I was glad to be released from the torments of the night and hoped for a beautiful day and that the sun would warm me up. Until the men woke up, I walked back and forth along the riverbank and breathed in the fresh morning air. The morning mists hovered over the river, which was no more than five meters wide. The other side of the river looked similar to the side we were on, with a wide grassy bank, except that behind it rose a dam on which sparse bushes grew. It reminded me of a dyke by the sea. The sun lifted the mist and it became clearer. Just a few meters away stood the tent where no one had moved yet. A line was stretched between two trees with men's stockings hanging from it.

Christian was the first of the two to wake up and nudged Jörg: "Wake up, you sleepyhead!"

He got up yawning without saying a word.

"Shall we take a look inside the tent?" asked Christian. But Jörg just stretched and stretched.

"He's a real morning grouch," Christian whispered to me.

I had to grin. We crept up to the tent carefully. Once again, the men threw small stones at the roof of the tent. But it remained quiet. Christian carefully opened the zipper and looked inside. The tent was empty.

"Great," he remarked, "and we idiots were sleeping outside in the cold."

"At least you slept," I said.

We looked at two inner tents containing air mattresses and woollen blankets. There was a camping table with used dishes in the anteroom. A suitcase lay on the ground.

"Maybe they were people who had spent their last night here and had long since left for Hungary. Maybe it's straight ahead, across the river to Hungary."

Jörg opened the suitcase. Strangely, there were only newspapers inside, presumably in Slovakian script. It didn't look like a crime had been committed here, nor did it look like anyone from the GDR had run away.

"Is there anything we can use?"

"Don't touch anything!" said Christian.

Jörg was about to pocket the breakfast knife that was lying on the dirty plate.

"If they do catch us, you'll have a gun on you and you'll get two more years!"

"But there's a pair of combination pliers."

"Okay, you might need these if there's barbed wire at the border."

Jörg pocketed the pliers.

"Look, there's a boat on the other bank!" shouted Christian.

"We should swim across and bring it here," I said, "then we can load our things into it and cross over on dry feet. I think we could wash ourselves again anyway. I haven't been able to wash for four days."

"And we haven't for a week."

We put our clothes down near the tent as if we owned it and jumped naked into the water. I brushed my teeth and soaped myself up. As the water washed over my body, I felt refreshed and swam to the boat on the other bank.

"Give me a hand!" I shouted and untied the rope from the peg to which the boat was tied.

"Unfortunately, we don't have paddles," Christian realized.

"Never mind, we'll just use our arms as paddles. It'll be fine."

Together we pushed the canoe through the water to the other side.

We hurriedly dried off and got dressed again. There was a loud rumbling in our stomachs.

"I'm starving," moaned Jörg.

"Then catch yourself a bear! We've run out of food," replied Christian, who was the first to get dressed and had already strapped his sleeping mat onto his rucksack.

"I still have a piece of bread," I said and divided it up.

It was no more than a dry slice for everyone, but it was better than nothing.

"It wouldn't be bad if we could buy something somewhere. We'll have to see what it's like on the other side of the river."

Jörg was just gathering his sandals when a man in work clothes, with boots and a cap and a dog appeared on the opposite bank, at the top of the embankment. He looked like a local. He watched us suspiciously and then climbed down to the bank. He stopped at the peg where the boat had been moored a short time before. He looked right and left across the river and disappeared again. We looked at each other questioningly.

"Strange, what was that," said Jörg, who was now sitting on the ground and fiddling with the buckle of his sandals.

Christian said: „Du musst zuerst den Nippel durch die Lasche ziehn und mit der kleinen Kurbel ganz nach oben drehn."[37]

He had finally managed to fasten the buckle. He stood up and wanted to grab his rucksack. The man with the dog we had just seen on the other bank suddenly appeared a few meters away from us. He opened the tent and came out again with paddles. Then he hurriedly jumped into the boat with the dog, which we were actually about to use to cross the river. He paddled to the other side and tied the boat back to its original place. Then he climbed up the embankment and disappeared from our sight again, along with the dog and paddle.

"That's a bad theatrical performance now, isn't it?" said Jörg.

"If you'd hurried more, you idiot, we'd be over there now," replied Christian.

"Could I have guessed that some clown who owns the boat was coming?"

"Stop arguing, it's no use," I shouted between them.

At that moment, the man reappeared on the other bank of the

---

37 A comedic song by Mike Krüger.

dam, followed by a herd of bleating sheep that the dog was driving forward.

"Wait a minute!" shouted Jörg. "Something's not right. How could he suddenly appear on our side without a boat? He didn't walk across the water like Jesus! And where did he suddenly get all those sheep?"

He ran past the tent where the river made a bend, came back and threw himself on the ground laughing.

"Are you completely crazy now?" asked Christian.

"Nah, but look around the corner!" He couldn't stop laughing. Just behind the bend in the river was a bridge over which a road led.

"Oh well, pretty funny."

We crossed the bridge and could still see the shepherd some distance away, walking along the banks of the Ipel with his sheep. The road that led over the bridge went straight to Sahy-Homok.

"I hope we find a baker soon," said Jörg.

Sahy-Homok

The sky soon clouded over again. Only occasionally did the sun peek through a hole in the clouds. The tarred road to Sahy-Homok led past green meadows and bushes. Soon after the bridge, the river Ipel was no longer visible. It had turned off somewhere. A mountain range rose up to our right, it must have been the Börzsöny Mountains (Pilsen Mountains) that we had seen on the train timetable. It started to rain lightly again. I pulled my hood over my head. All around, everything became gray and hazy. Visibility was no longer good. We soon arrived at the entrance to the village, where a road continued straight ahead. Strangely, a stretch of tarmac path turned off to the right and ended in the middle of the meadow. It looked as if it hadn't been finished. Behind it was an ascending wood.

We walked past the station building, which looked pretty deserted. Homok was written on the station sign. The door to the hall was open. There were no people to be seen for miles around. We walked along a gray wall, behind which the railway line ran, into the town, which consisted of a mixture of small old houses and new apartment blocks, wide roads and narrow alleys. Only a few people were out and about. Maybe it was still too early or they were all at work. We followed a street which, given the small stores and older houses, was most likely to lead to the city center. We needed something to eat and drink and information about the area. In a small store, I bought a large baguette, a salami, three bottles of water and three large bin bags.

"What do we need bin bags for?" asked Jörg.

Christian grinned: "For example, to put you in them and dispose of them."

I had to laugh: "Not a bad idea. But I was thinking more of using it as rainwear. We cut holes in it for our heads and hands."

"But we don't have a knife. I wish I'd brought the one from the tent."

"It's bad enough that you stole the shepherd's pliers."

"I've brought a pair of nail scissors," I said.

"Let's find a place to have breakfast first," said Jörg.

"It looks like a little park over there. Where there's a park, there are usually benches."

But it was just a park-like path. Behind it, we could hear people's voices and the sound of buses. We came to a large square surrounded on one side by beautiful medieval buildings and on the other by an elongated building that looked like a large warehouse. There was a bus station in the square with covered shelters and seating. I broke the baguette and the salami into three equal pieces. While we ate, we looked around. Many people crossed the square with shopping bags or waited at the bus stops. The buses pulled up to a stop, passengers got off and on, then circled the square and turned right a little further on.

"It probably goes to the border where the buses leave," said Jörg and took a bite of his salami. A young gypsy with cut-off jeans and a plastic bag full of things occasionally looked over at us in a friendly manner, which I took as an opportunity to ask him whether the buses go to Hungary from there.

„Mennek a buszok Magyarországra?"[38]

A bus had just left the opposite stop and drove past us. The friendly young man did his best. He suddenly ran like crazy after the bus to stop it. The bus actually stopped again and the driver waved us to hurry up. I was startled and signaled for the bus to continue, shouting:

„Nem bus, nem Magyarország!"[39]

All I needed was to get straight on the bus to Hungary and get caught at the border!

The young gypsy looked at me uncomprehendingly. The bus drove on.

"Let's get out of here quickly," I said. "It never occurred to me that the man would stop the bus. He completely misunderstood me. I had only asked if the buses were going to Hungary and expected a yes or no." We grabbed our rucksacks and hurried out of the square in the direction we had come from.

"There's no way I'm going to ask anyone here again," I

---

38 Are the buses going to Hungary?
39 Not bus, not Hungary!

remarked meekly. "We mustn't attract attention."

Christian said: "Maybe it was stupid of us to walk past the station. There's usually a map of the city in the waiting hall." We went back. There was indeed a map in a glass case in the station concourse. We could see from it that Sahy station was a few kilometers further north and that we were in Homok, a district right on the Hungarian border. From the bus station where we had been, it should only be a few meters to the border. Unfortunately, the map didn't show any details of the Hungarian side. "What do you think?" I asked. "We probably can't be any closer to the border. I think we need to think about how we're going to do it now."

We walked back to the bus station and then a little way down the road where the buses turned off. From a distance we could see the border checkpoint, a complex of buildings with barriers, gates and counters. There we crossed into Hungary. Several border police stood around a bus and checked it. The barrier finally went up and the bus drove on.

I took the compass out of my rucksack, calibrated it and said: "The border control house is roughly at the number 36. If we go a little further into the forest and keep following this number, we'll get to Hungary." We agreed to proceed according to this plan: I would lead the way with the compass. If I stopped, everyone had to stop. We didn't want to talk to each other during the escape and would run through the forest until we were sure we were in Hungary. If one of us was caught and the others still had a chance to escape, it was "every man for himself". We exchanged the addresses of our relatives, who were to be contacted in an emergency. Then we walked back through Bahnhofstrasse to the entrance to the village.

Border breakthrough from Homok

We crossed the level crossing and walked along the road that ended in the meadows towards the forest. A man in uniform looked after us from the railroad hut. It wasn't clear whether it was a border policeman or just a railroad official. Just before the road turned off, we could no longer see him because of the fog. That reassured us, because then he couldn't see us either. It was an advantage that it was foggy. It wasn't pleasant that it was drizzling, but we made raincoats out of the bin bags, cut holes in them for our heads and hands and were thus protected from the wet. The grey color was probably also a camouflage color in the forest. There were signs close to the small wood on the rise indicating the border area and forbidding passage.

It was 4.00 p.m. when we reached the outcrop of the grove and were able to dive into it undetected.

At first we had to fight our way through dense thorny undergrowth. The bin bags only provided partial protection against the thorns of the wild raspberries. We scratched our hands, which were sticking out of the slits in the bin bags. We also had to be careful that the branches didn't hit us in the face. The undergrowth cracked underfoot. I led the way with the compass around my right wrist, which was set to 36. The men followed me in silence. Birds fluttered out of the bushes in front of us. We waited until everything was quiet again before moving on. After just a few minutes, we had to cross a paved path that seemed to be fairly well traveled. It looked like an old border road. We had to be extremely vigilant and make sure no one was around. I cautiously peeked out from between the trees and looked around on all sides. Then I made a typical hand gesture and we quickly ran across the path to disappear back into the thicket of the forest. Something big was suddenly waiting in front of us in the bushes. We didn't move. Then there was a crash, twigs whizzed through the air and a deer hurriedly jumped away from us. The higher we climbed, the thinner the forest became. The initial mixed forest with thorn bushes was followed by a forest of oaks and hornbeams. The forest floor was covered with leaves, mosses and ferns. Dark scree peeked out from time to time. The shoes slipped. Jörg in particular had difficulties with his sandals, which were completely unsuitable for mountaineering. All my attention was focused solely on mastering the situation at hand and did not allow for any other thoughts. Every single step required the full concentration of all my senses. As soon as I heard a suspicious noise, I stopped. Jörg and Christian did the same. Conversation only took place in eye, facial expression and gesture language. I had to keep looking at the compass. My gaze wandered along the compass needle, to the direction of travel number 36 and from there to a prominent target in the area, a tree, a spot of light, a stone, a spring or whatever else seemed suitable, and we moved towards it. We climbed higher and higher into the mountains. Just a few meters ahead of us, the same serpentine path appeared several times, seemingly leading around a mountain cone. But we seemed to be climbing up the direct steep path to the top. At one point we heard the sound of an engine. A car was approaching. We pressed ourselves firmly onto the forest floor behind large trees. I could feel my heart racing. The jeep drove past. Border guards had been sitting in it but probably hadn't noticed us.

After we had been walking for about an hour, it became lighter above us. We could see the cloudy sky. We had reached the highest point of the mountain and a swath several meters wide opened up in front of us, similar to a flight path. This had to be the border. There was no fence here, no barbed wire. It was just as we had expected. So Jörg didn't need the pliers he had in his jacket pocket. I carefully pushed my head forward so that I could take a look at the aisle. Startled, I backed away, turned to Jörg and Christian, put my finger over my mouth and made a stern face. They understood: "Extreme danger!" To my left, about fifty meters below the mountain, I had discovered a guardhouse in the lane with a border guard standing in front of it. He was smoking a cigarette. His gaze first wandered over the trees in the forest opposite, then he slowly turned his head to the right. Fortunately, I had recognized his intention in time and was able to pull my head back. When I looked for him a second time, I saw him from behind, with his rifle shouldered, walking further downhill and disappearing into the fog.

I immediately gave the signal and we ran as fast as we could, crouching down across the lane. A huge ravine opened up in front of us and the descent was extremely steep.

We tumbled downhill more than we walked. Slippery, stony scree slithered behind us. We would certainly have been easy to spot from above, as the patchy old beech and oak trees let in plenty of light.

We ran from tree to tree with outstretched arms and had to be careful not to injure ourselves if we tried to catch ourselves on the trees while running fast. Only my subconscious took in the wild, untouched nature. Somewhere a woodpecker was hammering. We heard birds twittering, a slow worm hid behind a stone. A fire salamander slid down the scree with Jörg, who had slipped. The compass told me that we had to run towards rocky slopes. When we got there, we took a short breather and started talking to each other again in whispers.

"Where are we now, in Hungary, still in Czechoslovakia or is it no man's land? Is there going to be another swathe like that? Is it like the Berlin Wall? Are we perhaps in the middle of it?"

I could only shrug my shoulders: "I don't know. But there's no way we can feel safe. We have to keep walking until it's clear that we're in Hungary. So, for example, if we discover Hungarian garbage, disposable cans or something similar. I think we are still in the middle of the danger zone."

We were surrounded by rocks and large boulders that had probably broken away from the rock above us a long time ago, or perhaps they were volcanic bombs that were now overgrown with moss and lichen. Under the shelter of the rocks, we took a sip of water from the bottle and ate some of the baguette.

"There must be caves all around here," said Christian.

A spring gurgled out of a crevice in the rock and it looked as if a buried passage went into the mountain behind it.

"Unfortunately, we don't have time to find out. Maybe there's a bear in there too."

"That would be even worse than a border guard."

"Let's keep going instead."

We were halfway up a huge mountain cone and looked down into a wild valley with a wide stream. Fallen trees lay just as they had fallen years ago. Beyond the valley, the path climbed steeply uphill again.

"Do we really have to cross the stream and then go back up there?" asked Jörg.

"No other chance."

Christian and I had already managed to balance over a tree trunk lying across the stream and were waiting on the other bank.

"Look there, a dipper." Christian nudged me.

A small songbird flew over the water and suddenly dived under. A few meters further on, it shot back up out of the water and flew away. At the same moment, Jörg slipped off the slippery tree trunk and plopped into the stream. "Bloody hell! I could have walked right through it." He waded through the stream, splashing. His raincoat was torn to shreds, his trousers were soaking wet, the back of his trousers were muddy and his knees were green with moss. The sandals made smacking noises with every step.

"My God, now I know what a forest gnome looks like!" said Christian.

I tried to stifle my laughter, but I couldn't manage it.

Jörg waved me off: "If it's fun for you, I'm a forest gnome."

He opened his rucksack, which had fortunately remained dry, and took out a pair of training pants, which he put on. He rinsed the wet, muddy jeans clean in the stream, wrung them out and tied them to the outside of his rucksack so that they could dry. It had stopped raining and the mist had disappeared. We continued through the mighty wild valley with its babbling springs and fallen moss-covered trees. The sun had managed to send its rays through the canopy just before setting. A mysterious magic was spreading. The light-flooded greenery above our heads seemed to dance in the infinite silence. Individual rays of sunlight penetrated the treetops down to the forest floor and seemed like divine signs. I thought I had to hold my breath in awe. More mountains rose up around us, mostly with large stands of old beech trees. Our route first led us along the foot of a mountain cone, then it went uphill again. We walked in silence, one behind the other, until the forest opened up in front of us and a clearing could be seen, shimmering purple with willowherb and foxglove.

"Looks like a park landscape," Christian said.

But as soon as we stepped into the clearing, I whispered: "Back into the forest!"

From our cover, we saw a watchtower at the end of the clearing, similar to a hunter's post. A border guard was standing at an observation post. Fortunately, he had turned his back on us. We were probably still in the middle of the border area, but we didn't know whether it was a Czechoslovakian or Hungarian soldier. But it didn't really make much difference. Both would arrest us.

We quickly went back into the forest. We still kept to the marching direction number 36. Under the protection of the tall old trees, we first went uphill again on slippery lava-like ground and then steadily downhill again after a while. We probably had to constantly climb entire mountains whose height we didn't know and couldn't estimate. We just kept going forwards. We weren't trained mountaineers and didn't have any helpful equipment. Sometimes we had to shimmy from tree to tree or pull each other up by the arms. It was already getting dusk when we suddenly noticed a long strip of light ahead of us and assumed that we had reached another boundary route. Special attention and caution were required.

But how surprised we were when the supposed border lane turned out to be a well-concreted road. A forest path turned off to the right and another led straight on into the forest again. The concrete road turned left and there were signs with Hungarian text at intervals. I couldn't understand everything, but I concluded that it was a hiking trail. Beaming with joy, I shouted: "We're in Hungary! We've made it! I feel like I'm in a fairy tale."

"Sure, like in Mother Hulda[40] and you're the golden girl!" said Jörg.

"Then you're probably the unlucky one!" giggled Christian.

All the tension fell away from us. We marched along the road without a care in the world. A stream, whose name we didn't know, babbled alongside the road. Every now and then we passed a small house, a memorial plaque and once even a mill with a water wheel. The only thing we didn't encounter was people. Everything looked like a museum mile or a theater set.

"I hope we come to a real village soon," I said.

"It would be good to know where we are anyway."

The sun had set and it was getting dark. The road went on forever and then split. We decided to continue to the right, heading east.

If we'd had a map of the area, we would have been spared some bad decisions. The road eventually became a forest path and led back up into the densely wooded mountains. A waning half moon only sparsely illuminated the path. The sky above us became a section just as big as the forest path. All around us was dark night. Apart from the crunching under our feet, nothing could be heard. A mysterious silence surrounded us. We had been on our feet for eight hours and needed somewhere to sleep. But sleeping on the ground was impossible.

Although it was still summer, the nights in the mountains were very cold. We didn't know how high the mountains were, but the higher we climbed, the colder it got.

---

40 Frau Holle, a children's fairytale.

Tuesday, 29.08.1989: In the middle of the Börszöny Mountains
It had now turned midnight. We decided to walk to the top
of the mountain. Maybe from there, even though it was dark,
we could get a better view of the landscape and possibly
recognize a place.

When we reached the summit, however, we realized that as
far as we could see, there was nothing but mountains lined
up next to each other. But directly below us in the valley was
a huge sea of lights.

"That must be a city," Jörg remarked.

I said: "It reminds me of the view of Bratislava."

But Christian had his doubts: "I was already in the army. It
looks like a military camp to me, all barracks."

Despite our tiredness and doubts, we decided to carry on
towards the sea of lights. The closer we got, however, the
fewer lights there were. Soon we were surrounded by dark
forest once again. When we thought we had spotted a solitary
farmstead, we headed towards it.

But what a shock we got. Less than 100 meters ahead of us, in
the light of a lantern, we could clearly see an open barrier
with a soldier standing in front of it with a rifle over his
shoulder.

"Oh no, we have to get out of here!" whispered Christian.

Whether we wanted to or not, we had to make our way back
as quickly as possible. We almost voluntarily marched into a
Hungarian army camp. The soldiers there had orders to
secure their borders and also to pick up and hand over refugees from the GDR.

When we had initially decided to flee through the mountains,
we had assumed that the most difficult route would also be
the safest. We had managed to cross the border and knew
that we were in Hungary, somewhere in the Börszöny Mountains.

But how were we supposed to find our way back without a map or help from people? It was more difficult than we had imagined. Apart from the border police, from whom we had to keep our distance, we hadn't seen any other people. We hadn't come across any villages or settlements. The entire Hungarian army was probably stationed in the Börszöny Mountains. We had never had such an idea before. We had chosen not only the most difficult but also the most dangerous route.

"The mountain range must be huge and stretching eastwards with ever higher mountains," said Christian. "That would take us over the mountains for days."

"You're right about that. We have to go back and find the concrete road again. We have to go a bit north there. There must be a road to Budapest somewhere."

The forester's lodge
The thought of the military camp and the cold drove us on. We walked back through the dark forest all night like dream walkers. Shortly before 8.00 a.m. we arrived at the same place as the day before, at the concrete road and the two forest paths, one of which ran to the right and the other straight ahead.

The day before, in the gathering darkness, we had paid no further attention to the two forest paths and had continued along the road. But now, in the early morning, when the sun had risen, we thought we couldn't believe our eyes. Less than twenty meters ahead of us stood a house in a small clearing, brightly lit by the sunlight.

We watched from a distance as a woman came out of the house with a laundry basket and hung bed linen on a long line. The laundry fluttered slightly in the sunlight.

"Mrs. Holle!" whispered Christian. "This can't be true! We were joking about it yesterday!"

"Let's go to the woman. Maybe she can help us," I said.

The woman, who must be in her mid-fifties, was startled at first when three people approached her.

I tried my best with the few words I knew in Hungarian: "Jó napot kívánok. Bocsanat, az NDK-bol származunk"[41].

The woman made a sympathetic impression, looked the three of us up and down and seemed to understand immediately that we were refugees in a very difficult situation. She must have noticed that our clothes were dirty and that we looked tired and exhausted. I explained that I could only understand and speak a little Hungarian. The woman made an understandable hand gesture and we followed her into the house. We stood in a kitchen that resembled a long corridor. The woman pointed to the tap where we could wash our hands and fill our empty water bottles. She was probably very sympathetic and felt the need to help, because she handed us each a cup of hot latte and some kind of milky bread roll. Then she pointed to the wall clock and excitedly announced that a border police patrol came through the forest every morning at 8 a.m. sharp. That was a great danger for fugitives. We absolutely had to be out of the forest before 8.00 am. But we wouldn't be able to do that on our own. But her husband would be along shortly to help us.

Just a few minutes later, a jeep actually pulled up in front of the house. It was the husband in forestry uniform. "Gyors! Gyors!"[42] he said and made hand signals for us to get into his car quickly. A conversation was not possible. He tried to get us out of danger and out of the forest as quickly as possible.

41 Good day. Sorry, we are from the GDR.
42 Quick! Quick!

In a bend, on the opposite lane, a police jeep suddenly came towards us. The forester could only shout: "Maradj lent!"[43] and make an understandable hand gesture. Then the two jeeps drove past each other.

I had noticed how he greeted the patrol by holding his hand to his head. He drove on as quickly as possible. After a few more bends in the road, he stopped and pointed to the left, where a path led into the forest. "Gyors! Igy"[44] was all he said. We jumped out of the jeep. He drove on and we ran down the narrow path through the forest.

Without the help of the foresters, we would probably have wandered through the forest for a few more days or been shipped back to the GDR. Unfortunately, we didn't even have time to say thank you, let alone find out the names of the forester and his wife.

The farmland island

The narrow path led us out of the forest and an open, flat meadow landscape spread out before us. Only the occasional tree could be seen. A dirt track led to a road, which was probably the continuation of the road the forester had driven us along in the jeep, and also the one we had walked along for some time, always believing we were on a museum mile and out of danger. The police patrol should have spotted us long ago. We had probably been incredibly lucky so far.

The road seemed to lead to a neighboring village. It was still a few kilometers away, but we could already make it out dimly. Perhaps there was a train station there and a connection to Budapest. However, I didn't know whether I could still pay for tickets for three people. Perhaps it was also better to go unnoticed.

43 Stay down!
44 Quick! That way

We had now been walking continuously for more than 16 hours, more than two marathons. The tiredness made my feet leaden and my yawning never-ending.

Then we discovered a small island of farmland to the right of the road, surrounded by bushes and trees. This could be a good place to sleep. The field island had a pleasant depression so that we could lie there well protected on soft grass. The sun warmed the ground. We put our things down and were soon fast asleep.

We must have slept for three or four hours. It was lunchtime and after the many hours we had spent walking around freezing, the warmth felt good.

We didn't exactly look clean and tidy. Our pants, jackets and shoes were covered in mud from walking around on the mountains and the wet forest floor.

In the meantime, however, the sun had warmed and dried everything, including the jeans Jörg had fallen into the stream with.

"We have to clean our clothes, otherwise we'll stand out on the way," I said and took a small hand brush from my rucksack. I immediately started scrubbing away the dry mud splashes on my trouser legs. Surprisingly, it was successful. Jörg took his toothbrush out of his luggage and cleaned his clothes in his own special way.

"What's up?" he asked as Christian and I grinned at each other.

"I haven't needed the toothbrush so far anyway, have I?"

Christian teased: "I bet you'll clean that dirty brush again, won't you? Then you can brush your teeth with it again later!"

He asked me for my hand brush and cleaned his part of the equipment. When we all looked reasonably clean again, we decided to carry on to the next village.

We walked along the long straight road. Some distance away, we saw a railway crossing.

"That's a good sign!" exclaimed Christian.

"We can walk on the railway tracks for a change."

"That would also be an option."

Just as we were about to cross the level crossing, the barriers went down and a police jeep stopped next to us. I felt my knees start to tremble and the primal instinct to run away in case of danger kicked in. Christian and Jörg seemed to have noticed my excitement and took me into their midst. Minutes passed without anything happening or a train in sight.

"Just stay calm! If they had wanted to, they would have caught us long ago," whispered Christian.

At some point, the train arrived and the barriers opened again. The jeep turned off to the right, squealing, without the occupants even glancing at us.

The village of Drégelypalánk was still a few kilometers away. But ahead of us was a busy road that must have been heading towards Budapest.

On the way to Szentendre

"Maybe we should try hitchhiking," I suggested.

"I don't know if they check at the stations and whether we'll even have enough money for tickets."

"Who's going to stop for two guys and a woman?" Jörg objected.

"Maybe you'll give us the thumbs up and the two of us will hide for now," said Christian. "Women have more success on their own."

We walked alongside the road for a while. A few vehicles drove past us. But then a truck stopped and a friendly young driver let us in. He spoke some German and expressed his

160

sympathy for the current changes. Christian and Jörg took a seat in the second row, where the sleeping area was. We were able to ride as far as Szentendre.

The journey took about three hours. At the beginning we drove over valleys and hills and sparsely populated parts of the Börszöny, then the driver changed roads shortly before Vác. We reached the Danube Bend and the lowlands. Sometimes we could catch a glimpse of the Danube. The Pest region was quite densely populated.

The driver tried to give us some advice:

We shouldn't think that we could just get through the border to Austria. It would be better to go to the FRG embassy. On August 19, hundreds of GDR citizens had been able to escape in Sopron when the foreign ministers of Hungary and Austria (Gyula Horn and Alois Mock) cut the border fence together, but afterwards the border controls were tightened again. One refugee is even said to have been shot at the border strip.

The foreign ministers of Hungary and West Germany were now looking for solutions.

Shortly before Budapest, we drove over a bridge to the other side of the Danube. The driver stopped in Szentendre, wished us good luck and drove on.

We had heard the truck driver's words, but we still had to think about it. Should we give up so easily? Wasn't it better to try again to Austria? Would the politicians even find a solution?

Szentendre

It was already late in the afternoon when we walked through the pedestrian zone of the famous artists' town. I had visited Szentendre with Julia years before. This time, however, we weren't here to see the sights or buy anything interesting, like most tourists.

We walked hurriedly through the town, past many pretty stores, colorful houses, hotels and cafés. We ignored the artists who were painting pictures and offering to paint our portraits.

I had read the exchange rates for crowns and forints in the window of a bank. I still had Czech money that we could no longer use. It would be good if I could change it into forints. But going to the bank was a risk. I might have to show my passport and then it would be discovered that I was in the country illegally. I stopped at a vegetable stall, took out my wallet and asked the vendor if he could change Czech crowns into forints. I wasn't used to bargaining and haggling. But the shopkeeper used his advantage and gave me far fewer forints than I would have received from the bank.

I was annoyed and disappointed. No, not all Hungarians supported the refugees. There were people who exploited the hardship of others. But I had no other choice and had to put up with the discrimination. At least we had enough money to buy three more langosch and three bottles of water at a stall, so that we could soothe our growling stomachs for the time being.

We left Szentendre in the direction of the HEV train station and actually wanted to take the train to Budapest. From a distance, we noticed two men stopping a passenger from boarding the train. The passenger resisted. It was not clear to us whether the two men were Stasi officers or whether it was just a derailed situation.

"Let's get out of here," Christian whispered.

We had almost made it to our destination and didn't want to take any risks at the end.

I said: "There's maybe another twenty kilometers to go, we'll make it tomorrow. It's best if we walk a little further and find somewhere to sleep."

At first, we followed the railroad tracks.

Szentendre was behind us and it had become dark in the meantime. Illuminated trains ran in both directions every few minutes.

When we came to a hilly meadow landscape, we decided to look for a spot somewhere there. But it wasn't that easy after all. There was always a small farmstead somewhere where one or more dogs were barking. Apparently it was customary in Hungary to leave the dogs in the garden at night.

Whether we wanted to or not, we had to keep walking. Every house we passed was guarded by a barking dog, which also cheered on its nearest conspecific. Soon the whole town was barking and howling. We were lucky that one of the angry beasts didn't jump over the fence to tear us apart.

Eventually we found a patch of meadow far outside a settlement, at the foot of a hill, where it was quiet. The night was balmy. With the thought of being in Budapest in the morning, we went to sleep. The stars and a thin crescent moon shone above us.

Wednesday, 30.08.1989: In the Buda Hills

It was unclear which hill we had spent the night on. However, it was not difficult to find out which direction we had to take to get to Budapest. The metropolis lay at our feet, surrounded by mountains and valleys. Even from a distance, we could see the Buda section with Gellert Hill and the palace on

Castle Hill, where the kings had once reigned. The course of the Danube was also clearly visible. We found a downhill road and followed it along small rows of houses. The further we got into the plain, the more the traffic increased. Tourist buses drove past us. But of course we weren't going on a sightseeing or museum tour. Unfortunately, the batteries in my world receiver had given up the ghost and we could no longer receive any messages. But we had to assume that we would have to remain inconspicuous and cautious.

We discussed for a while whether it would be better to go to the West German embassy or get through to Austria ourselves. Once we had crossed the Czechoslovakian border, it must have been even easier to get to Austria. So far, all we knew was that the German embassy had closed and it was uncertain whether they were willing or able to help the GDR refugees at all.

I had to think about Julia. Zalaegerszeg was not far from the Austrian border and she and her family knew their way around the area.

To Zalaegerszeg

While we were still standing indecisively at a bend in the road, a small van pulled up next to us. A middle-aged man in blue work clothes got out, opened the back door and took out a bag. On the back door was a kind of billboard with an address from Mohács, autójavitó. (car repair shop)

By chance, his eyes fell on me and he asked: "NDK?"

"Igen, NDK, GDR," I replied.

"Menekültek vagytok?" (Are you refugees?)

"Igen."

„Szeretnenk menni Zalaegerzegre."[45] b I claimed, although I hadn't even discussed this with the men.

It turned out that he spoke much better German than I did Hungarian. We got into his van. He had bought spare parts in Budapest and now wanted to pick up his son from his grandparents' house for the summer vacation. That wasn't far from Zalaegerszeg. "The Hungarians hope that the people from the GDR will soon be free," he said. "We have to say thank you to Gorbachev. He allowed the Hungarians to stop renewing the border fences to Austria."

We were on the road with him for almost three hours, drove past Lake Velence and passed through many towns on Lake Balaton, such as Fonyod and Heviz.

Just after entering Zalaegerszeg, I noticed the familiar mountains with the new houses on the left. Julia's house was up there. Her father had built it after Julia and Joszef got married. The two girls grew up there and Julia was now a manager at the Zalaegerszeg clothing factory.

We thanked the car dealer from Mohacs, who gave us his business card as a parting gift.

With Julia in Zalagerszeg

We walked up the hill on the winding road. At a bus stop, I asked Jörg and Christian to wait ten minutes. I wanted to prepare my girlfriend for the situation first and then I would come back and pick them up.

I stood in front of the pretty little house where the roses were blooming, took a deep breath and rang the bell.

Julia opened the door. "Jesus Maria!" Isa? Where have you come from now?" She could hardly believe it.

---

45 We want to go to Zalaegerszeg.

I briefly explained the situation and that there were two men waiting downstairs at the bus stop with whom I was on the run.

Julia and her husband understood the difficult situation, but they didn't know how they could help and whether they might even be held responsible for helping people to escape. They had only returned from Italy the day before and were not familiar with the political situation. They also had to pick up their two daughters from their grandparents in Debrecen tomorrow. But of course they wanted to help as much as they could.

I walked back to the bus stop and picked up Jörg and Christian. "Did you think I was going to let you down?" I laughed. "No, we trust you," said Jörg.

"And 100 percent," added Christian.

Then we all sat together in the living room, answered the Hungarians' questions and told them how we had managed to cross the Slovakian border. Julia served us a snack of fried chicken pieces, freshly baked white bread, tomatoes and peppers. Afterwards, we discussed the next steps together.

Joszef, Julia's husband, suggested that we take the car to Lucacshaza, a town not far from the Austrian border. Maybe there was a chance of getting through there. In any case, we wanted to have a look around first, similar to the Czech border, and then decide how to proceed. We were of the opinion that it would be easier at the Austrian border, as many others had already crossed it in the meantime.

Julia gave everyone a packed lunch and a Coke. Then the five of us set off in the car, first in the direction of Szombathely. After about an hour we arrived in Lukacshaza. The mountain range that separates Hungary from Austria, the Günser Gebirge (or Köszegi hegység), loomed in front of us. The mountains must be of a similar height to the Börszöny, I assumed, between 600 and 900 meters. If you looked to the right, you could see a well-traveled road leading up into the mountains to the Hungarian border town of Köszeg. Similar to the Danube in Komarno, the lights of a huge searchlight would rotate between the sky and the ground here in the dark. "The next Austrian town is Eisenstadt," said Julia. We got out of the car at the end of Lukacshaza. It was a depressing farewell. I had to think back to 1968. Back then, Julia and I didn't know whether everything would go well. We hugged each other: "Please get in touch as soon as you can so that we know. We wish you the best of luck."

Behind Lukacshaza: 1st escape attempt to Austria
Farmland stretched out on both sides of the highway, but mainly cornfields.

Ahead of us lay the mountain range we wanted to cross. Everything would be similar to the first escape. I would lead the way with the compass. But we had no idea what lay ahead of us. After a short time, an Austrian car stopped and a friendly young man asked: "Would you like a lift? I'm going to Austria?"

"Thank you, but we don't want to go to Austria," I replied.

"We just want to see where the border is," Jörg added.

"Okay, I can let you out first," said the Austrian.

So we got in. The man asked where we were from and what we were planning to do. He had already guessed that we were from the GDR and wanted to escape. You could tell from the rucksacks.

There was no further conversation. Around a bend, a barrier with four Hungarian border guards and two shepherd dogs suddenly blocked the way. The driver had to brake hard and pull over. We were asked to get out of the car and show our

IDs. For a brief moment, I thought about running away. But that wouldn't have been a good idea. I could almost feel the dogs biting me on the rear. We didn't see the Austrian any more. Maybe it had even been his job to intercept refugees at the border. In any case, we had fallen for it.

The soldiers didn't speak German and a plausible conversation in Hungarian wasn't possible either.

We were asked to get into a jeep. Two armed soldiers sat opposite us and kept an eye on us.

Thursday, 31.08.1989: Szombathely Police Station

Twenty minutes later we arrived at the police station in Szombathely. All three of us were led into an interrogation room. A middle-aged Hungarian inspector with a gray moustache looked at our ID cards and compared the photos with our faces. Then he asked each of us in broken but understandable German: "What is your name? Why are you here? Do you want to go back to the GDR?"

I tried to get a picture of the man. He seemed calm and levelheaded and appeared to be a respected personality. I thought he looked like a younger version of Julia's father, probably because of the beard. He listened to the answers calmly and asked questions if he wasn't sure. Sometimes the corners of his mouth turned up into a smile. He seemed to sympathize with the GDR refugees.

The interrogation lasted an hour at most, but before it was over, the man stood up in all his grandeur and demanded with stern words and a raised index finger: "No more escaping! Hungarian soldiers protect the border well! Otherwise you go back to the GDR, then prison! Go to the FRG embassy in Budapest immediately! The Hungarian and FRG politicians negotiate for refugees! Do you understand?"

When we answered in the affirmative, he gave us back our ID cards and we were allowed to leave the station.

We were escorted to the station by a policeman and told to take the next train to Budapest.

On the way to the station, however, we changed our minds. Austria was less than 20 km away from here. We had seen the surroundings of Lukacshaza. Under no circumstances were we to rely on strangers again and run into the roadblocks.

We agreed: "If we're already here, we have to try again." We got on the train, but before it left, we got off again.

Second escape attempt to Austria

Just behind the large station building in Szombathely, we turned a corner to the right. Jörg said: "Wait a minute. I've got so much stuff in my rucksack, I don't want to carry any more." He pulled out his sleeping mat, which was in a plastic bag, and stuffed a few broken socks and underwear into it. Then he left everything against the station wall.

It wasn't long before the city was behind us. The plain with meadows and fields stretched out in front of us, continuing up to the mountains. It was mostly tall cornfields that provided shelter. The searchlight in Köszeg, high up on the mountain, was a good guide. We could also clearly see the road that led across the border to Austria. The bright headlights and the red tail lights of the cars showed us exactly where to go.

I set the marching direction number that would take us across the border at the appropriate distance from Köszeg. Then I went ahead, always with the intention of staying under cover. Christian and Jörg followed me.

Most of the time we walked through cornfields. When the field was over, I looked for the nearest hiding place, a hut, a bush, a dip in the ground. Then, crouching down, we would run as fast as we could to this target, pause for a moment and run towards the next object we had targeted. The surroundings seemed to be deserted. Only once was someone walking a dog in the distance. But that didn't seem dangerous. By now the sun was setting and it was dusk. This could be an advantage, similar to the fog in the Börszöny Mountains.

We had bypassed Lukacshaza and the roadblock and managed to get into the forest unnoticed.

We estimated that we were about 5 km from the road to Köszeg and were traveling parallel to it. We no longer passed through villages or settlements and there were no paths or trails. We went over mountains and valleys. At one point we reached a deep, wild valley and had to cross a small stream, then we climbed steeply again.

By now it had become very dark. I could no longer see the hand in front of my eyes and of course I couldn't see the compass either. We just kept going and came to a mountain cone, which was illuminated by the faint moonlight. Suddenly we were standing in front of a large, stately house, a multi-storey villa surrounded by a meadow. All around was quiet. No dogs were barking, no lights were on in the house.

"Are we perhaps already in Austria?" asked Christian. "It looks so civilized here."

We tried to find out anything. But there was no sign or doorbell on the house.

"This would be a nice place to sleep," said Jörg.

"Of course it would! But maybe this is a police station?" replied Christian.

"As nice as it would be here," I said, "let's move on. I was actually expecting to come across border fortifications or the remains of them at some point. We're probably still in Hungary."

We left the beautiful spot on the hilltop. There was no view over the mountains. There was nothing but black night all around us.

We walked further and further down the mountain. The beautiful house was long behind us. The closer we got to the valley, the more overgrown the surroundings became. We soon reached the bottom of the valley and were surrounded by black mountain walls. We could no longer see anything. We carefully trudged on along a muddy, rutted path. It was pretty certain that we were walking through deep vehicle tracks. Suddenly our path was blocked by a double row of wooden posts, some of which still had barbed wire hanging from them. We had arrived at the border fortifications.

"What are we going to do now?" whispered Christian.

"I don't know," I replied. "I don't know whether we're still in Hungary or already in Austria."

We just kept walking between the border fences. Maybe there was a place somewhere where you could be sure which side Austria was on. Without a map and light, there was no other solution. We trudged on in the dark, one of us putting his hand on the other's shoulder. It was slippery underfoot. We didn't know how long we could go on like this.

Suddenly, debris shuffled down the slope on the right. Immediately afterwards, shots rang through the air and flares lit up the darkness.

Then we were already surrounded by several border guards. Flashlights flashed.

"Állj meg!"[46]

"Hol van Ausztria?" I asked, which was pretty pointless under the circumstances, because I didn't get an answer.

The Hungarian border guards didn't speak a word of German.

---

46 Stop, stand still!

Instead, they tried to bombard me with questions that I didn't understand. I was only able to make it clear, speaking in German, that we were all three from the GDR and wanted to go to Austria. (Mi vagyunk NDK-ból. Ausztriába szeretnénk menni.) The soldiers didn't seem to believe my assertion that I only understood a little Hungarian.

The situation was almost ridiculous. The Hungarian border police, barely older than Christian and Jörg, lighted the way and politely asked us to get into the jeep.

Then we were transported back to Szombathely.

In the meantime, the sun was rising and a new day was dawning.

Friday, 01.09.1989: Szombathely Police Station again

We were taken back to the interrogation room. Strangely enough, the same police officer was sitting behind the desk as the day before, to whom we had promised to report to the German embassy in Budapest. His working day must have just started. He looked well rested.

But he didn't seem to believe his eyes. He rubbed his grey moustache thoughtfully between his thumb and forefinger and looked at us, one by one, at length. Then he spoke with a stern face: "You all back from yesterday?" "Sit down!"

It was a strange atmosphere. Everything seemed like a spectacle. This man couldn't really be malicious.

He only seemed to be playing this role because he had to.

He said loudly and insistently: "That's the end of the border! To Budapest! Or back to the GDR next time! Hungarian and German politicians negotiate now, Gyula Horn and Genscher, do you understand? Wait in Budapest at the German embassy!"

His face brightened up again and he looked at Jörg: "This is yours, yes? You left it at the station yesterday! Take it with you!" He handed him his plastic bag with the sleeping mat. Christian and I could hardly hold back a laugh and the Hungarian police officer laughed too. Then he became serious again, made a long arm and pointed to the door: "To Budapest!"

We left the police station. This time we gave up. We were unlikely to succeed in breaking through the border again, at least in this area. And perhaps we had got off lightly for the second time. Another police chief might have sent us back or arrested us. We didn't know what to believe. Perhaps the politicians had already negotiated.

After all, it wasn't a situation where thousands of GDR refugees were running around in Hungary.

What was to happen now?

"We have no more money for three tickets to Budapest," I said. "And we can't go back to my girlfriend in Zalaegerszeg either. We'd be standing in front of a locked door. They've just travelled to Debrecen."

"Then the only option is to hitchhike," Jörg concluded.

Hitchhiking to Fonyod

From the police station, we walked to a crossroads and then on to a well-travelled road that must lead out of the city. In front of us was a wide, flat landscape of sunflowers and corn. There was no village to be seen for miles around. Only the occasional tractor or car drove past us. After I had tried in vain to stop a lorry, an Austrian car in which a woman and a man were sitting suddenly stopped. The woman asked in a Viennese accent: "Are you refugees? Can we give you a lift?" They wanted to go to a meeting in Fonyod. It turned out that they had travelled from Vienna via Köszeg and Szombathely. Her name was Andrea and she was about 30 years old. His name was Marko, he was perhaps in his mid-50s and a Catholic priest from Romania who was temporarily living in Austria. They were not a married couple, as we had initially assumed. Both were very interested in what was happening in Hungary and shared a few news items. At the time, the Hungarian Foreign Minister Gyula Horn was in East Berlin negotiating with the GDR government. He wanted to give the refugees in Hungary the chance to leave via a third country, including Austria. It was not to be expected that the GDR government would agree. Hungary demanded that the Germans take responsibility for their compatriots and find a reasonable solution. For this reason, there were also negotiations between Hungary and the FRG government under Helmut Kohl. In the meantime, Hungarian Prime Minister Németh had publicly declared that no more GDR refugees would be extradited and that his country was prepared to provide accommodation for the refugees until a final decision was made. The Malteser and other aid organizations would take over the care.

The refugees no longer needed to be afraid that they would be handed over. But they still had to be careful, because there were still Stasi people in Hungary trying to persuade the refugees to come back.

When we got off the train in Fonyod, the two of them gave us a few forints so that we could buy tickets to Budapest. Andrea gave everyone a business card and said: "Please contact me when everything is behind you."

The train from Fonyód to Deli Pu. (South Station) Budapest took more than two hours by 2nd class train.

We used the time to get some sleep. We had been living like vagrants for more than a week, had hardly eaten or drunk anything and had never seen a bed or a shower. Our escape was a grueling game of cat and mouse, constantly hiding to avoid being caught and always hoping that there was a chance to escape. It turned out to be a mistake to think that it was easy to cross the Hungarian border into Austria. The border controls had actually been tightened. We were stuck, but it couldn't go on indefinitely as it was now. We were depressed and exhausted and unable to help ourselves. And like us, tens of thousands of people were now waiting in Warsaw, Prague and Budapest for relief from their hopeless situation.

01. and 02.09.1989: West German Embassyin Budapest
With the last money we had, we took a cab at Deli station.
"Német Nagykövetség!"[47], I said.
The cab driver nodded kindly and said: "Értem, Izso Utca"[48],
He took us across the Elisabeth Bridge. We could see the citadel with the Statue of Liberty from a distance and then arrived at the German embassy on Izso Utca about thirty minutes later in an incomprehensible zigzag. The cab driver drove off and we stood in front of a white wall with a locked wrought-iron gate, above which hung a plaque with the German eagle and the embassy address. Behind it was the embassy building, a kind of white double villa with three floors and a single wooden balcony with impressive carvings. There was a doorbell on the wall next to the gate.
After the bell rang three times, a man in a signal-colored jacket came to the gate. He belonged to the Maltese aid organization. We showed him our GDR ID cards and he let us in. We were taken to a room on the ground floor of the building, where we explained to an embassy employee why we wanted to leave the GDR. Then we filled out an application

47 German embassy
48 I understand, Izso Street

for a West German passport.

From the street side, we couldn't see that there were any other refugees. But when we got to the back of the house, we saw numerous people chatting on the lawn and two large tents with the Maltese cross. Most of them were young men and women or families with children. The tents reminded me of my childhood at vacation camp. I couldn't tell how many people were actually in the embassy, I estimated around a hundred. But the tents wouldn't fit that many.

Nevertheless, we were given woollen blankets to spend the night.

The people who belonged to the aid organization came from Hungary and West Germany. They took on all the necessary tasks, distributed food and drinks, handed out blankets, took care of reception and forwarding and answered all questions as far as they could. We learned that there had been many difficulties in recent months. Sometimes the embassy had to be closed due to overcrowding.

The first GDR refugees had been taken in by the Catholic priest Imre Kozma, who had opened a camp at Zugliget Church. As it was quickly overcrowded, a second camp was set up by the state in the pioneer village of Csillebérc. When this was no longer sufficient, a third camp was set up in Zanka, on Lake Balaton, also a pioneer camp.

In the meantime, tens of thousands of refugees were supposed to be in Hungary. Those who now came to the embassy were redirected to Zanka. The people we spoke to on the embassy grounds were mostly hopeful and believed that it couldn't be long before the way to West Germany was clear.

September 03, 1989: Provisional passports from the embassy
In the morning, shortly after breakfast, we were asked to collect our temporary passports from the embassy building. Step by step, we made our way through the long hall with rows of pillars on either side. The room looked a little gloomy due to the dark wood paneling on the walls. But the mood of the people was hopeful.

When it was Christian's, Jörg's and my turn, we were inspected from head to toe. Each of us was given a temporary green passport identifying us as citizens of the Federal Republic of Germany, a ticket to Zanka and a reasonable amount of pocket money. Jörg got off particularly well with the pocket money.

"My God," said the embassy employee, shaking his head: "What's that on your feet, are those supposed to be shoes?"

The sole of the right sandal had come loose and Jörg had mended it with a piece of insulating tape he had found on the way. The buckle on the left sandal had been replaced with a double knot made from sack tape.

"Those used to be my favorite sandals," Jörg replied somewhat meekly. "I'd love to buy a new pair, but ..."

"That's understandable," said the embassy official, handing him a special voucher so that he could buy new shoes.

When he looked at my shoes, he just said: "All right" and handed me the minimum bag money. There were no complaints about Christian's shoes either.

I had to laugh when Christian made a dippy face and said: "I wish I'd worn my old slippers on the run."

But then, of course, the joy of the temporary green passport issued in Budapest on September 3, 1989 prevailed.

03.09. to 11.09.1989: Pioneer camp Zanka

Before we went back to the deli station, we did some shopping on the way through the city center. Jörg actually bought a new pair of shoes. This time he opted for sneakers, which was a better choice. He also managed to leave his plastic bag of old clothes in a rubbish bin by the roadside, which he had failed to do in Szombathely. Now he added the old sandals. Christian really needed an iron ration of rusks to stop his stomach growling. I got batteries for the world receiver, paper, envelopes and stamps.

Fortunately, we had seats on the train from Budapest to Zanka and if we had been normal holidaymakers, we couldn't have wished for a better journey, a 2½ hour ride, past Lake Velence, through the royal town of Székesfehérvár and along Lake Balaton, mostly with a view of the lake. We were somehow ready for a vacation, but our minds could not rest. Now we were to wait in a camp without knowing what would happen next. We had tried to find our own way. But our escape to Austria had failed twice. Now, for better or worse, we were dependent on the decisions of the politicians. Towards evening we arrived at the train station in Zanka, a small town surrounded by vineyards. It wasn't difficult to find the former pioneer camp, now a refugee camp, because the way there had been signposted as a precaution.

The camp leader of Zanka was informed about other arrivals from the German embassy. After we had identified ourselves, we were allocated sleeping places in long barrack-like buildings, separately for men and women.

The aid organizations, the Maltese and members of the Red Cross, did a tremendous job here too. It was amazing how well everything was organized, the food and drink supply, the sanitary facilities and washing facilities. More refugees arrived every day, so that there were soon 2000 in the camp. Everything was very quiet. Even the children didn't make any noise or shout too loudly. They ran across the lawn or played with each other. The weather was pleasantly warm. There were long queues at mealtimes, but that didn't bother anyone, you talked to the person in front or behind you until it was your turn. Different meal times were set so that not everyone had to queue at the same time. Everyone was just grateful to be fed. Everyone could only praise the work of the emergency services.

Although the days went by without any results, there was growing confidence that the Hungarian government would soon find a solution.

As Jörg, Christian and I were now staying in different accommodation, we lost track of each other a little. Everyone made new acquaintances and gained new impressions.

We chatted, went down to the beach together, played cards or somehow killed time.

It was wonderful weather for swimming. Unfortunately, I didn't have any swimwear with me and it wasn't possible for me to go into the water in my underwear like the young men. So I sat down on the grass near the water and wrote letters and cards to my children, my brother, Julia and Ibrahim. There was a letterbox in the camp.

The camp management advised the refugees not to leave the camp. They were safe here. Outside the camp, there were still Stasi officers trying to persuade GDR citizens to come back.

It was undisputed that on August 21, a GDR citizen was shot dead at the border while trying to escape to Austria.

I couldn't help thinking that Christian, Jörg and I had walked between the barbed wire in the middle of the death strip. Luckily nothing else had happened to us. Only the border guards had arrested us.

Now that I had time to think, I began to wonder whether I would have been better off staying at home. The fact that I had managed to make it this far despite great difficulties was perhaps amazing, but not necessarily a reason to be happy. If I hadn't met Jörg and Christian in Komarno, I would certainly have gone home again. Now I was separated from my children without knowing how they were doing and whether they were getting into trouble because of me. They had probably reported me missing, because they had to let my school know. I had promised Frank that I wouldn't put myself in danger, but could I have guaranteed that? My children didn't know whether I had made it or whether I was even still alive. I wondered whether they had received the postcard from Komarno or whether it had been confiscated. We could only hope that everything would turn out all right. When my brother went to the West in 1961, 10 years had to pass before we saw each other again. And then it was the day of our mother's funeral. We couldn't foresee how the political situation would develop.

Other refugees were here with their whole family, with children or friends. They were very happy. Many of them had relatives waiting for them in the West.

I also had my brother and his family and many other relatives there. But I was worried about how they would take my escape. They probably wouldn't understand. To them, I was probably a ravenous mother who had abandoned her children. But the opposite was true. In order to continue to be there for my children, I had to leave. There was no other choice. I had experienced enough to know what consequences awaited me. I would break mentally. My life would be over. It didn't make sense for me or my children.

I very much regretted that we hadn't found time to talk to each other beforehand and look for a solution together. But there had simply been no opportunity to do so. It was the vacations and I had hardly seen my daughter in the last few weeks. She had been traveling a lot with her boyfriend. We were all convinced that there had to be changes. But I hadn't had any time to think about future life in the GDR. It was about my own life.

Monday, 4.10.1989: News in Zanka

Most of the people in the camp were young men, but there were also many families with children and some middle-aged people. Everyone had their own reasons for wanting to leave the GDR. They were neither hooligans or violent criminals nor people seduced by capitalism who came together here. Every single one of them had come here of their own free will.

The young people's thirst for adventure prevailed. Many had run away carefree. They had not yet seen anything of the world, but if there was an opportunity, they wanted to take it. The reasons varied. It was about family reunions, better working and living conditions, letting their children grow up in freedom, getting to know the world, escaping the paternalism and surveillance of the state.

But being free and deciding their own lives was what they all wanted. They came together here in the Zanka camp and hoped to come to West Germany, find work soon and build a new life for themselves, a life according to their own ideas. They had left everything behind and were ready to start all over again with nothing but their own strength.

On September 4, there was exciting news in the camp that spread like wildfire.

"Foreign journalists who had traveled to the Leipzig Autumn Fair reported in the media about a demonstration in Leipzig. Around 1200 people had taken to the streets and demonstrated. On placards they demanded human rights, freedom to travel and an open country with free people. When state security officers tried to break up the gathering by force and snatched the placards, the demonstrators shouted: "Stasi out!"

This had never happened before in the GDR. We thought about it in the camp. Was this a good or a bad sign? Would civil war soon break out and tanks roll through the country? Could the Prague Spring happen again in the GDR?"

Christian said: "I don't think Gorbachev will send tanks. He didn't even have the border fences to Austria renewed. Honecker is sick and the people up there don't know what to do anymore."

Jörg agreed with him: "I think it's all being blown out of proportion. Things will calm down again. When we left, nobody opened their mouths. Leipzig is not the whole GDR."

I wasn't reassured by their opinions. I had to think about my children. After all, most of the Soviet troops were stationed around Berlin and our apartment was very close to a Soviet airfield. If there was unrest now, I wasn't with them.

I couldn't reach them from Zanka either. We didn't have a telephone at home and if we had had one, the Stasi would have found out about my whereabouts immediately.

The day before, I had written a letter to the children just to send a sign of life. I couldn't give a return address. It was uncertain whether they would receive my letter at all.

In my mind I heard Frank say: "You always worry too much, Mum. We'll manage. We're adults after all."

But I knew better: they both still needed me and I needed

them. I hadn't seen Sandra again before I left. That's why I'd left her the friendship ring. I wanted us to always be connected. But would she even understand that?

I kept seeing the image of me getting on the bus and leaving my son at the bus stop. He became smaller and smaller until he had disappeared from my field of vision.

In the refugee camp, I came into closer contact with a woman whose bed was next to mine. She was a little older than me and had come here with her husband and an adult daughter. She told me that she had another daughter, but that she and her husband had already arrived in the West two years earlier by applying to leave the country. In the meantime, there was a grandchild there, of whom they had only seen photos so far. The whole family longed and wanted to be together again. She said: "We couldn't and didn't want to put up with this situation any longer and decided to flee. If there's any chance at all of seeing each other again, it's now." I understood the woman very well and told her my story.

She hugged me and said: "I understand their fears. It's almost worse for them than it is for us. But don't drive yourself crazy. Just don't go back to the GDR now.

Just wait and see. We all have to be patient."

It was known that the politicians of Hungary, Austria and the FRG had secret talks. The extent to which the politicians of the GDR were involved was questionable. Positive decisions were expected from President Gorbachev and Chancellor Kohl. But if you can only wait and hope, the days become very long.

Christian, Jörg and I seriously considered whether we shouldn't try to get through to to Austria again. We had behaved like dilettantes twice. But maybe we could make the breakthrough the third time. We could prepare ourselves better and get a map of the area around Köszeg. What if we had to stay here for another three or four weeks or if there was no exit at all?

Fortunately, things turned out differently.

Sunday, 10.09.1989: Statement by Foreign Minister Horn
On the evening of September 10, all GDR refugees were asked to gather in the camp's large gymnasium. Expectations and hopes were very high.

When the camp leader opened the meeting, there was total silence. He announced that the Hungarian Foreign Minister Gyula Horn had made a statement on Hungarian television, which he now wanted to read out to us.

At the words: "The Austrian border will be free for GDR citizens from September 11th", 2000 refugees broke out in a thunderous cry of joy and lay in each other's arms. The sentence that no further formalities were necessary and that there was no longer any dependence on an exit application to the GDR authorities was completely lost.

The speaker had to wait a very long moment until everyone had calmed down again.

They were then told how the camp was to be dissolved. GDR citizens with cars were allowed to enter the country the next morning, on September 11, via the Austrian border crossings.

For the others, Austrian buses were organized on the morning of 12 September to take them to Grafenau in Bavaria.

There, everything else would be arranged and the onward transportation to other reception camps in the federal states would take place.

There was great joy in the camp. Anyone who had the chance to drive towards the Austrian border in a Trabi, Wartburg or other vehicle set off in the evening, as it was already possible to drive through after midnight.

The camp was in a mood for departure. People were packing, exchanging addresses and wishing each other good luck with their new start.

On my bed I found a farewell letter from the Breuer family, who were already on their way to their daughter and grandchild. They had taken the opportunity to travel with someone in the car. We had barely met and had already lost sight of each other. They wished me all the best for the future and to see my children again soon.

Tuesday, 12.10.1989: Dissolution of the refugee camp
In the morning, several Austrian buses stopped at the entrance to the camp. Austrobus was written on the sides of the buses. I had spent eight days here in the camp and was glad to finally be moving on. I knew many of the people now boarding the buses by sight and had exchanged a few words with some of them. For a moment, we had been allies. Now everyone would soon be going their separate ways again.
Everyone who got on was first registered on a list.
I looked around for Jörg and Christian, but I couldn't find them anywhere. Their names weren't on the list either. I was a little worried. Were we going to lose sight of each other at the end? We had spoken to each other last night in the hall. They actually wanted to go on the buses too. I had to get on so as not to hinder those who were moving up. If they were on one of the other buses, I might see them again later. Somehow I had grown fond of them. After all, we had stuck together well, coped with difficult situations and had a lot of fun. The age difference no longer mattered. We had become friends. I couldn't lose them now!
The dissolution of the camp was a great event, not only for us refugees, but also for the Hungarian population. Humanity

had triumphed. We refugees were just as proud of this as the Hungarians. They shared their joy at the peaceful outcome with us. It gave us all a good feeling that better times were dawning, that governments would act more humanely in the future.

Word quickly spread about the route the Austrian coaches were to take. The convoy of 10 buses was impossible to miss. Many locals stood enthusiastically at the side of the road, waving and cheering at us in the buses as if we had achieved something great.

I waved back. But I didn't feel like a heroine. For me, they were the heroes themselves, the Hungarian people, the aid organizations and the Hungarian government.

We GDR refugees had only shifted our problems to Hungary and forced a solution on the Hungarian and West German governments.

Humanity had also triumphed thanks to Michael Gorbachev's glasnost and perestroika (openness and transformation). It was he who made it possible for Hungary to dismantle the border fences. We were now free and freedom was the most important thing in life. That meant: no more paternalism, freedom of opinion, human rights. It was possible to feel elated at these thoughts, a sense of victory.

But what did this victory mean for me personally? I had half a life behind me. It was clear that the other half would now have to start from scratch. In my backpack I had a notebook, a radio, a compass, a change of clothes, a pair of good shoes, a sweater, a skirt and a blouse. The bus had first gone in the direction of Sombathely and had left Hungary. We drove through Austria for a long time and finally crossed the Bavarian border at Freyung-Grafenau.

I thought of my children. When would I see them again?

Epilogue: What happened next

In the GDR, more and more people took to the streets and demanded human rights and freedom to travel.

I had already got a small apartment in my new home at the end of September.

On November 6, 1989, the doorbell rang at my apartment door. Unsuspecting, I opened the door. My son Frank and his friend were standing in front of the door. We fell into each other's arms, beaming with joy. The two of them had fled via Prague. Three days later, the Wall came down. We saw it on television, far away from home. Frank and I had found work in the meantime and I was able to buy an old but still drivable car at a reasonable price.

On December 24, 1989, Christmas Eve, we drove it back to our former home to see Sandra and Wilfried again. We had to take the transit route to West Berlin and were allowed to enter the GDR from midnight. A few hours later, we knocked on their bedroom window and woke them from their sleep. They had no idea we were coming. The joy of seeing them again was indescribable. Only now did we all realize what freedom really meant. We were reunited, spent the holidays and the New Year together and thought about our future together. We never wanted to part again.

THE END

Thanks

I would like to thank the following for reading the text of this book and for their constructive criticism:

Dörte Schuda

Sandra Bohnstedt

Thanks also to my husband, Peter Hannon, for his extensive literary support and research trips to the novel's locations.

Sources and literature

Berlin TouristenTips pocket-sized, 1986
Wikipedia: Division of Germany
Wikipedia: Wilhelm Pieck
Wikipedia: Walter Ulbricht
Wikipedia: Berlin Wall
Wikipedia: Erich Honecker
Wikipedia: Prague Spring
Wikipedia: Miklós Németh
Wikipedia: Mikhail Sergeyevich Gorbachev
Wikipedia: Pan-European breakfast
Wikipedia: Komarno
Wikipedia: Börzsöny
Wikipedia: Monday demonstrations1989
Wikipedia :Gyula Horn

Contents

Chapter IV - Escape..112

Contents...190

Gisela Bohnstedt-Hannon was born in Königsaue, Saxony-Anhalt, in 1947. After studying education in Halle/Saale, she completed a correspondence course in poetry/prose at the Leipzig Literature Institute and remained in the teaching profession until 1989, when she fled to West Germany. She later worked in the public sector as an employee in Nuremberg and Koblenz. She has lived in Münstermaifeld since 2002.

Books published:

Die Hasenodyssee
(*Ostermoor, Möhrenau, Greifenland*),
3 Children's books with CD,
Projekte Verlag Cornelius 2012

Der Vogelnarr,
Biographical novel,
Rhein-Mosel-Verlag 2020

Das Kind mit der rosa Schleife,
Novel, BOD-Verlag 2024